Adam was now

They both had agree... much more than ... beginning, a promise of more. Adam and she were made for each other. And so in time—probably not too much time—inevitably they would think of marriage. And, for him, that meant children.

It was a bitter irony. She had thought that she would never feel this way again. There was no chance that she would ever fall in love again. But she had.

The GPs, the nurses, the community, the location…

LAKESIDE PRACTICE

a dramatic place to fall in love...

Welcome to **Keldale**, a village nestled in the hills of the beautiful Lake District…where the medical staff face everything from dramatic mountain rescues to delivering babies— as well as the emotional rollercoasters of their own lives!

Visit Keldale again for Josh's story— coming soon in Medical Romance™

THE MIDWIFE'S BABY WISH

BY
GILL SANDERSON

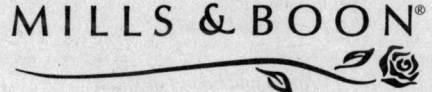

DID YOU PURCHASE THIS BOOK WITHOUT A COVER?

If you did, you should be aware it is **stolen property** as it was reported *unsold and destroyed* by a retailer. Neither the author nor the publisher has received any payment for this book.

All the characters in this book have no existence outside the imagination of the author, and have no relation whatsoever to anyone bearing the same name or names. They are not even distantly inspired by any individual known or unknown to the author, and all the incidents are pure invention.

All Rights Reserved including the right of reproduction in whole or in part in any form. This edition is published by arrangement with Harlequin Enterprises II B.V. The text of this publication or any part thereof may not be reproduced or transmitted in any form or by any means, electronic or mechanical, including photocopying, recording, storage in an information retrieval system, or otherwise, without the written permission of the publisher.

This book is sold subject to the condition that it shall not, by way of trade or otherwise, be lent, resold, hired out or otherwise circulated without the prior consent of the publisher in any form of binding or cover other than that in which it is published and without a similar condition including this condition being imposed on the subsequent purchaser.

MILLS & BOON and MILLS & BOON with the Rose Device are registered trademarks of the publisher.

*First published in Great Britain 2003
Harlequin Mills & Boon Limited,
Eton House, 18-24 Paradise Road, Richmond, Surrey TW9 1SR*

© Gill Sanderson 2003

ISBN 0 263 83438 7

*Set in Times Roman 10½ on 12 pt.
03-0403-48147*

*Printed and bound in Spain
by Litografia Rosés, S.A., Barcelona*

CHAPTER ONE

It was Sunday morning, and officially a day off, so midwife Lyn Pierce wasn't in her smart blue-and-white uniform. However, Lyn didn't pay much attention to days off. She had promised to call in so she would do so. Her work was her life—she had few other interests.

She looked down at one-year-old Edward Harris. Edward gurgled happily back at her, seeming the least concerned of anyone in the room. Behind Lyn were Edward's anxious parents, Bill and Julie. Behind them, and much more relaxed, sat Bill's mother and father.

Lyn reached down to pick up Edward, holding him to her with an expert hand. 'Edward is a wonder baby. I wish all babies were as healthy and as well cared-for as he is.'

'But we've never left him before,' Julie said. 'Since he was born I've never spent more than an hour away from him. Going away seems sort of uncaring.'

'Not at all. Don't be selfish. Let Edward's grandparents have a look-in. They certainly know what to do.'

'We ought to,' the grandmother said with a grin. 'We've had five children of our own and there are three other grandchildren.'

'I'm more worried about you and Bill than the baby,' Lyn went on. 'You've done a great job so far in bringing him up. Now you need a rest, a bit of self-indulgence. Getting away will do you the world of good.'

'Well, if you're sure,' Julie said slowly, 'we would like to…'

'I am sure, very sure. Now, get in that car, go away and enjoy yourselves.'

'All right, we will.' Julie had only needed a bit of reassurance and now she was suddenly quite determined. 'Bill, fetch the cases down, we'll get straight off.'

Lyn winked at the grandparents, and the grandfather winked back. 'I'll be off, too,' Lyn said. 'I know there'll be absolutely no need to call, but you have my mobile number.' She walked out into the sunshine.

Julie walked with her, now obviously delighted. 'I'm looking forward to this now. Bill's booked us into a hotel in York. I've packed clothes I haven't worn for ages. And it'll just be the two of us.' She suddenly looked shocked. 'Is that a terrible thing to say?'

'No, Julie, it isn't. Edward isn't the only person in your life. You have a husband to love as well. Now, go and have a good time!' Julie hesitated a moment and then left.

Lyn walked to her car, checking that her boat was safe on its trailer. Then she drove away. As she headed out of the village of Keldale, she remembered the excitement, the joys, the fears of having a baby. And the pleasure of sharing those joys with a husband. Then she shook her head and drove a little faster. Those thoughts were none of her business now.

She was driving to Lake Windermere, fifteen miles away. She loved it here in the Lake District at this time of year. The colours of the trees, lakes, sky and fields seemed different, more subtle in early autumn. Autumn suited her mood. She often felt autumnal, a little melancholy, as if the summer of her life was past. Then she shook herself. That was a foolish idea. She was a successful midwife, a career-woman of thirty-two.

Lyn parked at the sailing club, slid off her loose trousers to reveal shorts underneath. Her smart trainers were changed for a disreputable pair with the toes cut off to let water out. Then she enjoyed herself, erecting the mast, rigging her dinghy, bending on the sails. Finally, blue sails flapping, she wheeled her dinghy to the hard and pushed it into the water.

As she tethered it to a convenient bollard she caught sight of the name of her dinghy—the *Start Again*. Her shoulders hunched. Naming the dinghy had been a wild reaction against a malevolent fate. Sometimes now she thought it had been a little foolish. An over-reaction, perhaps.

Back at the car, Lyn strapped on her lifejacket, then took a carefully wrapped parcel of papers and placed them into a waterproof box. She dropped in her mobile phone and her handbag. In a dinghy, you expected everything to fall overboard. Then she returned to the dinghy, carefully strapped down the box and pushed off. This was what she had come for.

Carefully, she threaded her way through the other dinghies, passed visitors happily splashing in hired rowing boats, avoided the moored luxury cruisers. Nearer the shore the wind was erratic at first, but when she reached open water she found a stiff breeze that cracked open the sails and made her little craft heel. This was good!

She sat out further, listened to the hiss of water under the stem, felt the heat of the sun on the back of her neck. This north end of the lake was ringed by mountains, she could see the grey blue summits all around.

Now she was away from other people. She was happy.

Lyn tacked across to the west bank, turned to run along it to where she had been told there would be a large motor cruiser moored. After fifteen minutes she saw it—there was the blue superstructure, the flag indicating that it had been hired from the boatyard.

As she saw it her boat heeled again and automatically she let air spill from the sails. A cold wind chilled her back and when she glanced over her shoulder she saw the dark line of a squall hastening towards her over the water. This was the Lake District, where the weather could change in half a minute. No matter, she'd soon be at the cruiser.

She was calling on Dr Adam Fletcher. In a fortnight he was going to join the Keldale practice for six months while one of the other partners was on a training course. Lyn wasn't looking forward to working with him.

Just yesterday, when she'd accepted this job as water-borne postman, the senior partner of the practice, her friend Cal Mitchell had said, 'It'll raise the profile of the practice, Lyn. A real, live, television star. Just what we need to show how good we are.'

'We don't need a television star to prove we're good. We've got the opinions of our patients. That's all that matters.'

'You don't want to work with a TV star?'

She knew Cal had been teasing her.

'I want to do my work and be left alone! That's all.'

Cal had lifted a hand to calm her. 'I interviewed him myself. I think he'll be a good man. He has excellent references—medical ones, not from TV, from people I trust. And I've watched a couple of his programmes. I think they will help people.'

'And don't tell me—he looks absolutely wonderful.'

'Yes, Lyn, he does look wonderful. But he's still a good doctor. You have to give him a chance.'

She trusted Cal's judgement. 'Whatever you say. I'll give him a chance. Now, what is this packet I have to deliver?'

'Just if you happen to be on Lake Windermere tomorrow. And you said you were. He's hired a cruiser for a bit of peace. He wants to do some writing and some studying before he starts with us. I've told him there won't be much chance afterwards. But this packet came for him and it looks important. I'd just like to get it to him to show him that we're a practice that helps each other.'

'OK, I'll do it,' Lyn had said. But she wasn't looking forward to the job. She wasn't expecting to like the new partner. She didn't like successful, good-looking, flamboyant men. Not that she thought about men much at all.

The wind was now growing stronger. Suddenly there were whitecaps to the waves and she found herself feeling cold. But she felt confident. She was a competent sailor, she could deal with this. She needed to be competent at everything she did.

So far there was no sign of life on the cruiser ahead. Presumably, the doctor was writing or studying below decks. She was now almost alongside, and calculated that the best thing to do was to cut across the stern of the cruiser and come up on the shore side. There it would be sheltered, she could tie her dinghy to the side of the cruiser cockpit and climb aboard.

She put her helm up, the dinghy careered across the cruiser stern and just at that moment the strongest squall so far raced across the lake. The dinghy heeled, water sloshed into it and she stretched and leaned backwards to jerk it back onto an even keel. She could hold it…just. But then there was a loud crack.

No time for fear or panic. She knew her mast had snapped, knew that the sail would fall. The dinghy lurched upright and she was catapulted backwards. There was an instant's shock as her body dropped into the cold water. Then a sudden blinding pain in her head. And then there was blackness.

Lyn's head hurt. She had been asleep, now she was waking up. Her head hurt and if she came thoroughly awake then her head would hurt more. She wanted to stay asleep, she didn't want to wake up and hurt even more. But she didn't seem to have any choice.

Her eyes she kept carefully closed. What else did she know? She was warm, but some bits of her were damp. There were other pains apart from that in her head, and her right thigh hurt. She was lying on her back, more or less comfortable. How she wished she didn't have to wake up. She couldn't help it. She groaned.

A voice said, 'You're waking up. Just lie there. You've had a nasty crack on the head but I think you're going to be OK.' It was a deep voice, a soothing voice, a comforting voice. She wanted to do what it said. But instead she opened her eyes. Just where was she?

To her side was a brass porthole so she was on a boat—presumably the cruiser. Lyn turned her head and saw a shelf with a row of medical books. She looked downwards. There was a sheet and a blanket—and, suddenly, something else struck her.

'Who undressed me?' she asked.

'I did. I thought it necessary. You were cold and wet and I wanted to look at your thigh to see how near that cut was to the artery. Besides, I am a doctor.' The voice was reassuring but not apologetic. 'Now, I'd like to look in your eyes.'

His hands were gentle on the side of her head and Lyn stared upwards, not paying much attention to the face so close to hers. Of course, she knew what he was doing, checking for signs of concussion. Then she blinked and twitched, a cold drop of something having fallen on her face. 'Sorry,' he muttered, and added, 'Pupils are the same size. I don't think there's any need for you to go to hospital. But you should rest for a while and then I'll see about stitching up your head.'

By now she was more conscious, able to think about what had happened, to take in her surroundings. 'You're wet,' she said.

'I certainly am. I had to jump in to pull you out, you were floating away. There I was, quietly working, when there was this great thump on the stern. I came into the cockpit, thinking that I had a visitor. And I had, but she was unconscious.'

She'd think more about that later. 'My boat! What happened to my boat?'

'I've tied it to the side of the cruiser. No problem there but you're going to need a new mast.'

'I see.' Lyn's headache was getting worse. 'Can you tell me what happened? I was rounding the stern of your cruiser and my mast snapped so I... What happened then?'

'You fell backwards onto the cruiser's propeller. It gave you a nasty cut.'

She struggled, tried to sit upright. 'The box! There were papers for you in a box and I—'

Gently, he eased her back to the pillow. 'I found the box. It's on board and we can worry about it later. Now, apart from the head and the thigh, are there any other aches or pains? I had a quick look at you but I couldn't see anything.'

'My head's the worst, but I don't think there's anything much else.'

'You didn't swallow any water? I think I got you out in time.'

'No, I'm not going to drown.'

'Then that's enough talking. Just lie there for a few minutes, there's no need to worry about anything. We'll sort things out later. I'll be sitting here, reading.'

He had a voice that inspired confidence, a deep voice that made you want to do what he said. She lay back, tried to relax and let her confused thoughts sort themselves out.

Her hair was still wet. He had put a towel underneath her head and she could feel the bulk of some kind of dressing as well. She was pleasantly warm, but there was some dampness and she realised that when he'd undressed her he'd left on her bra and panties.

Then she had to blush a little. Most of the time she dressed in her uniform or, when at home, in shirt and jeans. She didn't have much occasion to wear fancy clothes. But she had a secret vice. Her underwear was always of the finest, most delicate lace. Just the opposite of what would be expected of a sensible midwife.

Well, he had seen it. Let him make of it what he wished.

For a few moments more she lay there and then decided she was strong enough to talk again. 'Did you say you thought my head should be sutured?'

'I'd like to put at least one in. Head wounds bleed a lot but I don't think there's any serious damage.'

'Will you have to cut the hair away?' Lyn couldn't stop the note of anxiety in her voice.

He laughed. 'I very much doubt it. If I do it'll be the absolute minimum. Now, before we go any further, should we tell anyone where you are? Is anyone going to worry about you?'

'No one worries about me. I look after myself.'

She hadn't meant it to sound so defiant.

'I see. And did you say that you had some papers for me? How did you know I was here?'

She sighed. Now they would have to get professional, and an explanation would be required and so on. 'My name's Lyn Pierce. I'm the midwife at Keldale practice. And I know you're Dr Adam Fletcher. A parcel of papers was sent to you at the practice and Cal Mitchell thought they might be important. So, since I was coming for a sail on the lake anyway, I thought I may as well bring them to you.'

'That was very good of you. Midwife Lyn Pierce, I'm very pleased to meet you.'

He held out a hand and as she took it he noticed her ring. 'That'll be Mrs Lyn Pierce?'

'I hope it will be Lyn. And although I'm Mrs Pierce, I'm a widow.' Then she sat upright and looked at him properly for the first time. And he was sensational!

He had longish blond hair, still wet and now roughly pushed back. His eyes were large, but she couldn't tell what colour they were. They seemed an odd, indeterminate grey-green. His expression was concerned, thoughtful, but she thought there was humour underneath. And he was a big man! He must have changed because his clothes were dry, but the dampness of his body made the muscles show.

With a shock, she realised that she hadn't been so instantly attracted to a man in years. And it was mutual. Something passed between them, some consciousness that things had changed, that life would never be quite the same again. She saw his eyes darken, his expression change. He was as lost as she was. She let go of his hand. She had no idea how long she had held it.

She tried to find refuge in the ordinary. 'Well, I'm feeling much better now, Dr Fletcher, and—'

'It's Adam,' he said gently, 'and as your doctor I say that you aren't much better. I prescribe at least another half-hour's rest. I'll fetch you a couple of painkillers and you can lie here quietly. I'll go next door and read these papers you've been to so much trouble to bring. And you're sure no one will worry about you?'

'No one will worry about me.'

'Well, I think that's a pity.' He handed her a glass of water and two pills. 'Take these and try to rest.'

So Lyn took them, and did as he told her. Soon the throbbing in her head diminished. It was strangely peaceful, lying there. She could just detect the slight rocking of the cruiser, hear the splashing of waves against the hull. She glanced round the room—no, it was a cabin. She was in a bunk, a double one. There were clothes on a stool and she could see male toiletries on a built-in dresser. A dressing-gown hung from a hook. Obviously it was his bedroom and it felt oddly intimate.

What had happened between them? Why that sudden feeling that they'd known each other before? She must be more shocked than she'd realised. But there was no chance that she would sleep. She'd just shut her eyes for a moment, and then call to him and...

She seemed to have been asking herself this question a lot recently. Where was she?

Then recollection flooded back. The trip across the lake, the accident, the pain in her head that was still with her. And meeting Dr Fletcher...Adam. He seemed to be... How did she know he was standing just above her? She opened her eyes, and there he was.

'I heard your breathing change,' he said, 'I knew you were waking up so I brought you some tea. Want to sit up?'

Adam put his arm behind her, eased her forward and dropped a pillow behind her back—just like an experienced nurse, she thought. But as Lyn sat upright the blanket and sheet fell away from her chest, and she clutched them back to her.

Without changing expression, he threw her a large

tracksuit top. 'Wear this for now. It zips open so you don't have to pull it over your head. Back in a minute.' Then he left the room.

He's considerate, she thought as she carefully pulled on the thick garment. We both know he's undressed me, but he doesn't want to embarrass me. I think I like him. She reached for the tea he had left her.

When he returned he had her lean forward so he could lift the temporary dressing on the back of her head. 'Doesn't look too bad. I'd like to put a suture in, though, just to be certain. Now, ordinarily I'd ask a nurse to wash your hair. But I haven't got a nurse, so do you mind if I do it?'

'You wash my hair?'

'I don't want you to try to do it yourself. So either I do it or you stay smelling of lake and crusted with blood.'

'Did anyone tell you that you're a very persuasive man? Where do we perform this hair-washing?'

'I have a tiny bathroom. If we leave the door open, I think there might be room enough there for the pair of us.'

Lyn borrowed his dressing-gown and they decided that first of all she would have a shower. Then he passed through the rest of the tracksuit and she dressed, then sat on a tiny stool with her back to the washbasin. Adam was gentle, shampooing her hair and dabbing it dry. Then he decided that he didn't need to shave any hair away and could suture her cut quite easily. She told him she could put a plaster on her leg herself.

'What happened to my shirt and shorts?'

'They're in the cockpit, drying. You're not going to put them on?'

She waved at the basin in front of her. 'I thought I might make use of your facilities and do a bit of clothes-washing. If you don't mind?'

'Be my guest.' Adam fetched the garments and passed her a small packet of washing powder. This man was amazing!

She washed and rinsed everything, including her bra and briefs, wrung them out then carried them through to the cockpit. She felt a little uneasy, wearing no underwear, but consoled herself with the thought that the baggy tracksuit would hide the fact.

The sun was out again. The squall that had resulted in her capsizing had long passed and it was a glorious September day again. 'Do you mind if I turn your beautiful cruiser into a washing line?'

He waved an urbane hand. 'It'll make it seem more like a working boat. Spread your things on the deck, they'll soon dry. Then sit here in the sun and we'll get to know each other. And in a minute we'll have some lunch. Are you hungry yet? Cold water makes me hungry.'

'It would be nice to have something to eat.' Lyn realised that, yes, she was hungry. But her native caution asserted itself. What had he meant when he'd said that they would get to know each other?

While she'd been in the shower he'd somehow washed and combed his own hair. Now he did look like a TV presenter. There was something in his face that inspired confidence. She felt that whatever this man told her she would believe. He wasn't the kind of man she usually took to but, in spite of herself, she found herself liking him. And so she was wary.

She sat on the other side of the cockpit from him, having spread out her washing, and huddled the folds of the tracksuit to her body.

'It was good of you to bring those papers to me,' Adam said. 'They were quite important. I've got to go down to London tomorrow and I'm glad to have read them first. Now, would you like to dine in the saloon or shall we eat out here? That locker lid there cleverly converts into a table.'

'I'd like to eat out here. But may I help you—?'

'No need. I threw a few things together while you were asleep. Just sit there and recuperate and leave it all to me.'

He seemed remarkably efficient. Within minutes there was a table fixed in the cockpit, a cloth and cutlery on it. He served soup, which she suspected was home-made. To follow came a tossed salad, chicken and hot rolls. 'You did all this yourself? I thought TV presenters ate in expensive canteens and were taken out for posh meals.'

'That does happen sometimes. But once I was a penniless student, and I liked to eat well. So I taught myself to cook. There's not much difference in time or money between eating well and eating badly. I've got a fridge and freezer on board and every three days I call in for supplies. Now, more chicken?'

Lyn was enjoying herself. It was easy to ignore the dull ache in her head, to forget that she was sitting in a baggy borrowed tracksuit with no underwear on. She was enjoying herself because she was with this man. And he seemed to be going out of his way not to alarm her. There was no aggressive masculinity. He was content to sit and be with her.

'Why are you coming up here to work?' Lyn asked. 'We're a long way from the bright lights of London.'

'I'm a doctor,' he replied simply. 'It's what I love doing more than anything. Even more than making TV programmes,' he added with a smile.

'I'm afraid I've never seen one of your programmes,' she said, and found that she was genuinely sorry. 'I just don't seem to have time. But won't you be lonely away from your friends?'

'No. London can be a lonely place even though there are so many people there. I'm looking forward to something different.'

'You'll like the practice. We're like a family, we look after each other.' Lyn paused, wondering how to phrase the next question. She decided to be blunt. 'You're not married?'

Adam didn't seem to mind her frankness. 'No. Never have been and there's no one in mind at the moment. But I'm not against marriage. I just never met anyone... You said you were a widow? I don't mean to pry.'

She had told the story so many times before that she should have become used to it. But it was still hard. 'I was married for five wonderful years. And then three years ago my husband was killed in a farming accident. I think of him every day. But I have my work and that is very fulfilling.'

'I can imagine. You had no children? They can make a difference to even the saddest thing.' His voice was gentle.

'No. No children. I had a late miscarriage and there was never a chance again.'

Rather to her surprise, she thought that he was genuinely upset by her story. She could tell that he wanted to know more, but was too courteous to ask. And for the moment she didn't want to say any more.

When their meal was over, he again refused her offer of help. 'I'll clear away, I know exactly where everything goes. This won't take me five minutes.'

So Lyn sat out there in the sun, enjoying the coffee that he brought her.

And when he rejoined her she said, rather reluctantly, 'I suppose I ought to be getting back. Somehow.'

'No problem. You're still injured and you're not to strain yourself in any way. I've got your boat tied alongside, I've baled her out and unshipped the mast. I'll just tow her back to...where did you come from?'

'I'm parked at the sailing club. I can leave the boat there and arrange to have a new mast fitted.'

They both looked over the edge of the cruiser at the dinghy tied alongside. 'I've never been sailing,' he said. 'Is it fun?'

'It's fun and hard work. If you like, when I get a new mast I'll take you for a sail.'

'I'll hold you to that. Now, should I be towing you back?' Adam's face and voice were both bland. 'Of course, you've had a nasty knock on the head so it might be a good idea if you didn't drive straight away. If you don't have to get back, why don't you stay on board for the afternoon? We could go for a bit of a cruise, up and down the lake.'

'Don't you have work to do?'

'I do. But I fancy a rest. And I came up here for the scenery. I'd like to share watching it with someone.'

Lyn knew she ought to say no. But why not? It was

just a trip up and down the lake with a colleague. 'I'd love a cruise.' She smiled.

So Adam fastened her dinghy astern and they pottered down the quiet west side of the lake, admiring the views and trying to avoid the traffic on the east side. They passed the car ferry and headed for the centre of the lake, now blue and silver under the high sun. In the distance they could dimly hear the noises of civilisation—the rumble of traffic, the shouting of children in the chilly water, an occasional radio. But they felt alone. This was their own little world.

After a while Adam said that he would take her back now. How had he known that she had been thinking it was time they returned? But she said nothing. They headed back towards town and she saw the buildings growing bigger and thought that in a few minutes they would have to part. Her clothes were now nearly dry. Lyn went to the bedroom to change, rather sadly taking off the baggy tracksuit.

When they were nearly at the yacht club he hove to and she slid overboard back into her dinghy. She could paddle to shore from here. 'Thank you so much,' she called, 'I have enjoyed—'

'Not goodbye yet. I'll see you at the club in a couple of minutes.' Then he pushed the dinghy towards the shore.

He must have moored the cruiser at one of the jetties belonging to the boatyard, because five minutes later, just as she was arranging to have a new mast fitted, he turned up behind her, then walked her to her car.

'I'm sorry you hurt your head,' he said, 'but you've no idea how much I've enjoyed today.'

'I've enjoyed it, too.'

'Perhaps we could have another day out on the boat together?'

This was heading into dangerous territory. 'Perhaps,' Lyn said uncertainly, 'but I am kept very busy, you know. I don't have a lot of time.' She didn't know quite what else to say and her words came out more stilted than she'd intended. 'I'm glad to welcome you to the practice.'

'I'm glad to join it. It's nice to think that I've got at least one friend there already. Now, you know what head wounds are like—get yours checked.' Adam leaned forward, kissed her gently on the cheek. 'It's been a good day for me, Lyn.' Then he was gone.

The streets of the little town were busy and it took all Lyn's concentration to navigate the crowds of good-natured holidaymakers. But soon she was in the countryside, able to enjoy the scenery, to think over her day. She had a lot to think about.

After being pulled out of the water she had really enjoyed her day—she couldn't remember when she had enjoyed a day so much. She had felt an excitement that was new to her. Adam was such good company. He made her feel alive, he made her feel like a woman again.

Then she felt foolish. All that was between her and him was simple animal attraction. He was a good-looking, charming man, probably practised because of his appearance on TV. She had been vulnerable to his charm because of the injury to her head. She had to remember that she was a widowed midwife, happy and fulfilled in her career and needing nothing more.

Once she had been married. For five years she had been ecstatically happy—and then one afternoon her world had crashed about her. Her husband had left home one morning, and that afternoon he was dead.

She'd thought she couldn't survive the pain of that tearing apart. But somehow she had. And with survival had come a determination never to make herself vulnerable again. There was too much pain in love. She never wanted another man. Adam would be a friend—but nothing more.

She drew up outside her home, one of the row of little terraced houses owned by the practice. Her neighbour Jane waved to her and called for her to come in for a coffee. Jane was the district nurse, and engaged to Cal.

Lyn had plenty to tell her and when she had finished her story, Jane looked at Lyn's injured head and decided that Adam was very competent and there was no need for Cal to look at the wound that evening. 'Now, tell me what's he like.'

Lyn shrugged. 'He seemed pleasant enough. I think he's a good doctor.'

'He rescued you, fed you, took you for a trip round the lake and all you can say is that he seems pleasant enough! I want details!'

'I didn't really notice. I suppose he's good-looking and he's got a nice voice.'

Jane looked at her friend disapprovingly. 'You know you get a little black mark on your soul every time you tell a lie,' she said righteously.

It was getting dark now. Some twenty miles away Adam Fletcher was sitting in the cockpit of the cruiser, a glass of wine in his hand, watching the blood-red sun sink below the black line of the mountaintops. He'd had an interesting day.

Lyn Pierce. If he closed his eyes he could imagine her sitting opposite him in the cockpit, wearing his old grey tracksuit. Strange how such a shapeless garment could look so good! And before that, when he had pulled off her wet outer clothes, she had been…no, that kind of thought was unprofessional!

But one thing was certain. When she had opened her eyes, when they had first looked at each other, there had been a shiver of recognition, an instant attraction that both of them had felt. He'd felt it, he knew she'd felt it, too. But would she acknowledge it?

At first sight she didn't seem remarkable. Her face was pleasant, her figure trim. Her hair was cut short, close to her head. She seemed guarded. It had taken her a while to smile, and she tended to look downwards. Only after a while had she revealed herself. But slowly he had come to realize she was beautiful.

What of her personality? He suspected that, having been widowed so suddenly, it had made her lock down her emotions. She'd been badly hurt and it wasn't going to happen again. He knew she would be his friend. But if he indicated he wanted more than friendship, then what would happen? She would run.

Did he want to be more than just her friend? After all, he had only just met her. It would take time. But something told him that, yes, possibly, this could be the woman he had longed for so much.

How to persuade her of this?

CHAPTER TWO

'I GATHER you met our new doctor yesterday,' Cal Mitchell said to Lyn next morning. 'I also gather from Jane that you got a bit of a head injury. In my room—I want to have a look.'

'No need. Just one stitch and I feel...' But she followed him to his room anyway.

'It's a great job,' he said after a quick glance. 'I'll get Adam to do all our suturing. But it's the last time I ask you to act as a water-postwoman. Think you'll be able to work with him?'

'I don't see why not. Seems a good type.'

'Quite. Jane says that you went for a trip round the lake with him.'

Lyn shrugged, just a little uncomfortably. 'I'd hit my head. He said he wanted to keep an eye on me for a while to make sure that I was OK. I'm sure you'd have done exactly the same.'

'Certainly,' said Cal. 'I'd have done exactly the same.' She didn't know what to make of his deadpan face.

On Monday mornings she ran her parent-education class and then held the antenatal clinic. The surgery had a custom-built clinic, with all that she could possibly want to hand. To the side was her own small office, with her files and her desk and her own examination room. Cal believed that his staff could only give their best if they had room to manoeuvre. Everyone had their own desk, their own area of work and their own storage space. It didn't seem much, but she knew midwives who were much less lucky.

The parent-education classes were fun. They were as much a social occasion as a medical one. After a talk and the relaxation practice, the mums-to-be gathered together to compare notes, pregnancy outfits and gossip. Afterwards Lyn held the antenatal clinic and at the end of the morning she felt that she'd had a good time.

The afternoon was spent on her rounds, checking babies due and babies just born. She enjoyed this, too, visiting homes in villages, farms and little outposts.

'How much sleep do you get Jenny?' she asked a wan new mum.

Somehow, Jenny managed a smile. 'Not a lot. I'll swear that baby waits till I've dozed off and then starts to cry. I feed her a bit and then I wake up and she nods off. It's worst in the middle of the night.'

Lyn thought for a minute. It wasn't something she liked to recommend but... 'You could express some milk. Keep it in a bottle and then get your husband to feed little Mary. I take it he'd be willing?'

Jenny looked thoughtful. 'I guess he would. He's a farmer, he's stayed up all night to feed his new animals—why not his own daughter? You're sure it'll be all right, Lyn?'

'Perfectly all right. Lots of my mums do it. And you need your sleep.'

Yes, it was enjoyable work, it was her life. Though she had to refuse an awful lot of cups of tea.

When she got home that evening there was a brief message on her answering machine, saying that her mast would be replaced by the following Friday. She blinked at this. After talking to Cal that morning, not once had she thought about the events of the previous day or her meeting with Adam. Even when her head had itched a little, she hadn't thought about how she'd been injured. Why not? She wondered if she had unconsciously pushed Adam to the back of her mind, had decided just not to think of him. But why? Did he bother her that much? He was only a new colleague. Then she remembered that sudden flash of attraction and shivered.

Irritated with herself, Lyn put on the kettle and turned to her mail. There was a thank-you card from a new mum, saying the baby was doing well and that it all would have been a lot harder without Lyn's help. Feeling pleased, she put it on her mantelpiece. There were the usual advertising brochures, which she skimmed through and dropped into the bin. It struck her that she didn't get much personal mail. Her life was local, constricted. How many letters would Adam Fletcher get? Why was she thinking about him so much?

She was glad when she heard a knock on her door. It was Jane, with her niece Helen by her side. 'Just in case you're interested,' Jane said, 'Cal's just phoned me and asked me to tell you. On TV this evening, at eight o'clock, there's an awards show for the best documentaries. And our new doctor's getting one. I thought you might like to watch.'

'He said he had to go down to London today,' Lyn said thoughtfully, 'but he didn't say he was getting an award.'

'Obviously not a pushy type. Are you going to watch?'

'I might as well,' Lyn said carelessly. 'I've got

nothing much else to do and it'll be interesting to see a bit of one of his programmes.'

'This is the man who saved you from a watery death! I want a bit of enthusiasm. And he's good-looking!'

'Nothing at all to do with anything,' Lyn said insincerely. 'If I can't watch it, I'll record it.'

But as she closed the door she knew that she'd both watch and record it. She was looking forward to it.

It was time for her tea but she wasn't hungry. She felt vaguely uneasy. She didn't want to read, watch TV, listen to music. There was some washing to do, a bit of ironing, she could clean out the kitchen and check the oven. But as she performed these little domestic duties she knew they weren't helping. She didn't know what she wanted. Finally she made herself a sandwich and forced herself to relax.

Why was she so restless in her own home?

She had moved in here with her husband eight years ago, and they'd intended to buy their own place in time. But somehow it had never happened. And after Michael's death Cal had said that she wasn't even to think about having to move. Now she had her home just as she liked it. There was comfort in the rooms she had decorated, the furniture she had bought, the garden she had cultivated. She was happy here. But was it getting just a little constricting?

Lyn laughed. This mood would soon pass. She'd switch on the TV.

All it was was that she had quite liked Adam. Well, you had to feel something for a man who had fished you out of a lake and then undressed you. Now she was going to enjoy seeing him on TV and feel happy that he was getting an award.

No, she had to be honest with herself. She had felt more attracted to Adam than she had to any man since... since... All right, she would think it. Since her husband had died. But these things happened. The feeling would quietly die away.

There was a set of awards for a variety of programmes. But soon enough came the award for the best new medical documentary of the year. First there was an extract. It gave her an odd feeling to see on the screen the man she had been so close to the day before. He was talking about Alzheimer's disease and how it affected families and careers, and she thought he was good. More than good.

Lyn herself felt like clapping when Adam walked up to get his award. The black and white of his evening dress suited him very well.

When the awards were over there was a party in the studio, and a roving reporter and cameraman wandered round, picking out people to question further. Lyn wasn't surprised when they swooped on Adam. He was the best-looking man to win anything.

But then Lyn frowned. Who was that clinging to Adam's arm? The woman was tall and blonde, with a dress that showed what Lyn thought was an unnecessary amount of cleavage. She seemed to have a lot of teeth. Lyn didn't like her.

'Will you be making a further series of medical programmes, Dr Fletcher?'

'Possibly, but not for a while. I'm a doctor before I'm anything else.'

'I'll persuade him,' the blonde said, with an even more toothy smile. 'I'm sure I can.'

'I hope you succeed.' And the interviewer was on her way.

The programme finished shortly afterwards and Lyn switched off in some dissatisfaction. If the blonde was the kind of woman that Adam liked, then she didn't see the two of them having much in common. Irritated, she went to bed.

It was the Monday morning Adam was due to start work, and as many of the staff as possible gathered in the coffee-room to meet him. Cal thought these little get-togethers were very important and there was a lot of curiosity over the new arrival.

But Adam didn't arrive.

Cal looked round, then moved onto some other business they all had to discuss. After twenty minutes he frowned and checked his watch. Lyn knew he didn't like his staff to be late unless there was a very good reason. And she didn't think that this was like the Adam she had met.

Cal excused himself and went to speak to the receptionist. When he came back into the meeting he said, 'There has been no message from Dr Fletcher. I'm sure there's a very good reason for his non-appearance so we'll postpone the introductions until another time.'

His voice was calm and reasonable, but everyone there knew he was angry. He went on, 'There's another problem that we all have to face and that is—'

The coffee-room door opened and Adam walked in.

Lyn was unprepared for the glow of excitement she felt when she saw him. For a moment her life seemed more interesting, she was really looking forward to working with this man. Then she decided that reaction was foolish.

Looking more closely, she decided there was something wrong with his appearance. He was wearing a conventional dark suit, light shirt and sober tie—the usual garb of a senior GP. but it all looked rumpled, as if he had been running or lifting something heavy. And what was that yellow stuff in his blond hair?

Cal smiled, not a pleasant smile. 'Dr Fletcher, we've been expecting you for a while.'

Adam was equally calm. 'I must apologise for my lateness. I would have phoned but I'm afraid my mobile is now at the bottom of Lassiter's grain silo.' He paused and gave a wry smile. 'For a while I thought I might be there, too.'

Lyn squeezed her eyes in horror. Silos were great metal tubes, thirty or forty feet high, used to store free-flowing grain and other drystuffs. If a man fell in—as quite often happened—in certain circumstances he could be sucked down and suffocated. It was quite a common cause of death in rural areas.

She looked round. Everyone was as shocked as she was. Cal looked very disturbed. 'I've warned Lassiter about that silo!' he said darkly. 'And this time I'll make sure that the health and safety inspector does something. What happened?'

Adam shrugged. 'I was just lucky. I was driving past the farmyard when I saw three men running toward the silo. It was obvious that something had happened. I stopped in case they needed a doctor. When we got to the top of the silo a man's head was nearly under the grain. The three men held my legs and I managed to grab him, pull him out a bit and then hold him till we could get a rope down to him and hoist him out. I managed to get most of the grain out of him and gave him mouth-to-mouth. Then the ambulance arrived.'

'Welcome to medicine in the countryside,' Cal said with a smile and shook Adam's hand.

After that the introductions were largely an anticlimax. There were a couple of other things that Cal wanted to discuss, and then the staff left for the morning's work, Cal having a last word with Adam.

Lyn collected her messages from the receptionist and was walking down the corridor when she heard a voice behind her. 'Lyn…how's the head?'

She stopped to speak to Adam. He moved towards her a moment to let a nurse pass behind him and she found being so close to him was unsettling. And did he wait rather a long time before easing back?

'My head's fine, thank you. As you said, I had Cal to check it. But how are you? That story about being upside down in the silo—it terrified me.'

'Just gymnastics, anyone could have done it. I didn't hurt my head, like you.' His concern for her seemed to be more than the usual concern of a doctor for his patient. He went on, 'No other ill effects?'

'None at all.' She didn't want to be reminded of how vulnerable she had been, and decided to move onto the offensive. 'I saw you on TV last Monday, but only by accident. Why didn't you tell me you were going to get an award?'

Adam shrugged. 'It's all in the past now.'

'We would have been interested.' Lyn knew that she shouldn't, but couldn't resist the next remark. 'Your blonde companion certainly made an impact. A good friend of yours?'

It had been a mistake. His expression told her that

he had guessed what she was thinking and she flushed.

'My blonde companion? Alice? I borrowed her for the evening. She's the wife of a doctor friend of mine, who for once in her life wanted to appear on television. Perhaps she got carried away a little.'

'The wife of a friend? But I thought that she was your...that is, you were...'

Now she was certain that he was laughing at her. 'Certainly not. I'm godfather to their first child but that's all. At the moment there is no lady in my life that I'm close to. I thought I told you that.'

'I must have forgotten. Now, I'd better get on with my work. I hope you'll be happy here, Adam.'

As she walked down the corridor she felt annoyed with herself. Why had she felt a little thrill of pleasure when she'd heard that the woman was only a friend? Adam Fletcher was nothing to her. In six months he would be gone.

As it was Monday, relaxation classes first and then antenatal clinic time. There were the usual observations to be taken, blood pressure, pulse and so on, palpation of the abdomen, urine specimens and the very necessary chat afterwards. Lyn tried to reserve a minimum of twenty-five minutes for each patient, but it wasn't always possible.

It all went well, all was as usual, but Lyn thought that one of her patients seemed a little subdued. Marion Parsons was already the mother of two lovely children and her obs were fine, but at thirty-two weeks her uterus seemed a little small to Lyn. She palpated the abdomen, felt the distance from the fundus—not quite enough.

Lyn thought for a minute. 'Marion, I'd like you to

go to hospital,' she said gently. 'Just for a check-up. I'll arrange it at once.'

But Marion had quite a way to come. It was hard for her to get to the surgery, never mind the hospital. 'Is it really necessary?' she pleaded. 'The other babies have all been fine. Can't we wait a while and see?'

'I really think you should go to the hospital,' Lyn said, 'but I'll see if we can get a second opinion. Perhaps we can squeeze you in with one of the doctors.'

She walked along to the reception desk.

'Dr Fletcher,' the receptionist said. 'He spent some time with Cal first, but Cal said it was pointless and he could see his own patients.' She reached for her pad and scanned it. 'In twenty minutes?'

'Great,' Lyn said. She dropped the bundle of notes on the desk. 'Patient is Marion Parsons.'

It would be the first time she'd worked with Adam and she was wondering what it would be like.

Lyn remembered how thoughtful Adam had been when she'd been injured, and he was exactly the same way with Marion. There were a few friendly words first to make Marion feel at home, then Lyn took her behind the screen to get undressed while Adam checked her notes.

After he'd finished examining Marion, he said, 'Fine. Just get dressed and we'll have a talk.

'I don't think there's any real cause for alarm, Marion,' he said when they were sitting by his desk again. 'However, the baby's growth seems to be a little retarded so we're going to refer you for a couple of tests in hospital. As well to be certain, isn't it? You should get an appointment very soon. Come back and see us next Monday and we should have the results. But don't worry. These things do happen.'

Marion looked worried. 'But it's had for me to get to the hospital, Doctor—it'll take three bus rides and there's the other kids to think of. Do I have to go?'

'We have to be certain, Mrs Parsons. I'll see if we can organize an ambulance for you.' He looked questioningly at Lyn. 'That should be possible, shouldn't it?'

'We can manage that.' Lyn nodded.

Mrs Parsons sighed. 'Well, that's a help. I must say, I feel better now. Thank you, Doctor, you've been very kind.'

It was Adam's last appointment so Lyn came back to see him after she'd seen Marion out. 'She was your patient,' he pointed out. 'You could have referred her yourself. You probably know more about this kind of thing than I do.'

Lyn was pleased that he could acknowledge this. 'Just calming Marion down a bit,' she said. 'I'm sorry if you feel that I was wasting your—'

'Good Lord, no! You were wasting nothing. Patients are entitled to reassurance, no matter where it comes from. There's much more to medicine than diagnosing and prescribing.'

She liked this idea. She found that she didn't want to leave the room; she wanted to stay to chat a while. He was an easy man to chat to. 'How have you enjoyed your first half day here?'

'I've enjoyed it no end. It's different, having a practice that's scattered all over the local hills instead of one that's confined to a few city streets. Perhaps I'll look for a permanent job here, never go back to London. I like the weather, the scenery.' He paused a moment and then said, 'I very much like the people, too.'

She didn't want to think too much about this. Hastily, she said, 'Wait till winter time. You might change your mind.'

'I doubt it.' He glanced at his watch. 'That seems to be the end of my morning session. Shall we go and have a coffee together?'

But Lyn decided that she needed a breathing space before she met him again. 'I do my rounds this afternoon. I think I'd better get off at once. See you around, Adam.' And she fled.

When she'd gone, Adam went to the window of his consulting room and looked out. There was a view across the lawn to a grove of great trees, and beyond he could see a line of hills, with distant white-painted farmhouses. Very different from the noisy streets outside his old London rooms. He was going to like working here.

Apart from his experience in the silo, he'd had a typical GP's morning. A patient with persistent backache—he'd decided it was muscular rather than anything affecting the kidneys. An embarrassed older woman for whom he'd prescribed medication for cystitis. An eighty-year-old man who'd really dropped in for a chat, but had been happy to be reassured and given a prescription for his chest complaint. A mother whose child could not shake off a cold.

There were no life-threatening diseases, nothing greatly exciting. But he was meeting people, helping them with their problems, making their lives easier. It was what he enjoyed.

The work was different from his work in the city. There was an expectation that there'd be a little time for a chat, that he was a person as well as a doctor.

A couple of his patients had taken over an hour traveling to see him—the practice was very widespread so people expected a little more than a quick diagnosis and prescription. They had social needs.

So, he liked the surroundings and the work. But it wasn't just these that attracted him. He'd just had his first professional encounter with Lyn. He knew he was going to work well with her. And he hoped they might become friends—or even more.

That evening Jane and Cal called on her, bringing Helen with them. They often called round as, being nextdoor neighbours, Jane and Lyn had become very close.

'We've got something to tell you, or ask you,' Cal said, holding Jane's hand. 'I've persuaded Jane to move into the house with me. We'll be getting married soon and it's silly her running between my house and hers. And Jane says my place needs a woman's touch.'

'And how,' said Jane.

'Moving in does make more sense,' Lyn agreed, 'and I'll be sorry to see you go. But what did you have to ask me?'

'How d'you feel about having Adam Fletcher as a neighbour? He's been renting a cruiser for a few weeks but at present he's lodging at the Red Lion. He's happy enough there but I think he'd like a place of his own. It's just that when you first heard he was coming to the practice you didn't seem too pleased.'

'He's not like I thought he might be,' Lyn said. 'In fact, I quite like him. I'm sure we'll get on well, though not as well as I've got on with Jane. But it was good of you to ask me, Cal.'

'Settled, then.' Cal grinned and looked down affectionately at Helen. 'Come on, twinkles, time to go home for supper.'

When they had gone Lyn wondered about what had been decided. She and Jane had been in and out of each other's houses, each other's lives, for the past few months. How would it be with Adam? There were another two houses in the little terrace, and she got on with the inhabitants well enough. But something told her that she'd see more of Adam.

She'd be living next door to a very attractive man, who seemed to have indicated that he found her attractive, too. She was half excited, half afraid. Then it struck her, with a force that was entirely unexpected, that if he asked her out—if he seemed to want to see more of her—she would accept. She swallowed. In half a minute her entire life picture, the way she saw herself, had changed. She was no longer Lyn Pierce, a widow. She was Lyn Pierce, a young, unmarried woman.

She swallowed. This would take some getting used to.

CHAPTER THREE

IT WAS typical of Jane. Once the decision had been made she had to act at once. Next evening she brought Helen round and asked Lyn to come and help them pack. Lyn went next door and spent an amiable hour wrapping paper round glasses, sorting out clothes, packing trinkets.

'Almost like old times this is.' Jane smiled as she folded up shorts and tops. 'I used to be constantly moving on—I could pack my life into a large rucksack. But I've got attached to this house. It's never happened before. And I know I'm going to love living with Cal. I've got plans for his place.'

'I shall miss you,' Lyn said.

'No, you won't. First of all, I'm only moving a hundred yards down the road. Secondly, there'll be a very handsome man living next to you.' Jane raised her eyebrows. 'Whatever you and I did together, it'll be more fun doing something else with him.'

'Jane!'

'Don't tell me you haven't at least thought of it. Now, it's time for a rest and a cup of tea.'

Lyn decided not to say anything more. Perhaps she didn't want to think about what Jane had said.

They were drinking their tea when they heard a car stop outside. 'That'll be Cal,' Jane said. 'Go and let him in, Helen.'

There was the murmur of voices at the front door. But it wasn't Cal who appeared in the living room, clutching Helen's hand. It was Adam. Lyn looked at him blankly.

'This young lady said I was to come in,' he said. 'I hope I'm not disturbing you.'

'No disturbance,' Jane said quickly, 'I'll pour you a mug of tea.'

Lyn guessed that he must have just finished evening surgery as he was still in his formal clothes. He said, 'I was just driving back to the Red Lion. But I'm rather excited about moving in here and I wondered if I could just put my head round the door. If it's inconvenient then I'll go at once and—'

'Of course it's not inconvenient. If you don't mind the mess, you can look round as much as you like.'

'And first you can see my new doll, Rosie,' Helen said. 'I'm Helen. What's your name?'

Adam smiled. 'Hello, Helen. I'm Adam. And I'd love to see Rosie first.'

Helen beamed. 'This is Rosie over here.' She stretched up her hand and Adam took it obligingly, to Jane's obvious delight.

'Someone's made a conquest,' Jane whispered. 'Don't you think he's gorgeous, too?'

Lyn didn't reply, knowing Jane liked being outrageous occasionally. Instead, she watched him and Helen. The two seemed to get on tremendously well.

After a while he rejoined them and Jane took him on a lightning tour. 'I'm very impressed,' he said. 'I know I'm going to be really happy here. And I gather you'll be my neighbour, Lyn.'

'I will. This must be different from your London flat.'

He looked round the living room, glanced at the French windows that opened onto a little back garden. 'Very different. Here I knocked on a half-open door and a little girl invited me in. In my London flat you ring the doorbell and I inspect you through my closed-circuit television before letting you in. I prefer this.'

He looked at Jane, and then at Helen, who was playing in a corner. 'I'm not quite sure yet who Helen is.'

Jane explained. 'She's the daughter of my sister and Cal's brother. They were both killed in a car crash a few months ago. So Helen was left an orphan, with just an uncle and aunt. And we decided to make her a home and get married. The three of us are happy and we're going to be happier.'

Adam turned to look at the little figure playing in the corner. 'Poor Helen,' he said. 'She's lucky, of course, having you and Cal, but poor Helen.'

Lyn realised that he was genuinely upset. She knew that doctors had to walk a thin line between caring and getting too emotionally involved. It was unusual to see one quite so moved. She thought she liked him for it. 'You like children?' she asked.

'Very much so. For a while I thought of becoming a paediatrician. Then I decided I preferred general medicine.'

Lyn could always trust Jane not to be afraid to ask awkward questions. And now she said, 'If you like them so much, why haven't you any of your own?'

His answer was thoughtful, honest. Lyn realised he wasn't trying to score points or be flippant.

'I've been taking my time. Perhaps I wasn't ready before. I think I'm nearly ready now. I'm not so busy now. When—and if—I have children I can spend time with them, enjoy watching them growing up.'

Lyn was a bit irritated, she wasn't sure why. 'And who's going to be the lucky mother?' she asked.

He didn't rise to her challenge. 'Not that I've found a wife yet but I'm…well, not exactly looking but hoping. Too many people get married too quickly and for the wrong reasons.'

Cheerfully Jane said, 'You sound like one of your own programmes. I'm sure I've heard you say something similar.'

He grinned. 'Very possibly. But it's true. After all, if it's been on telly it must be true.'

They all laughed. After a while he went on, more seriously, 'When I do get married I want to get it right, find the right woman for me.'

'Will you know?' asked Lyn.

Here again he seemed to ponder, to try to give an honest answer. 'I think I will. And I think the right woman is worth both waiting for and fighting for.'

He stood. 'Now I must go. I see you've plenty to do and I've been stopping you doing it. Lyn, I'm looking forward to having you as a neighbour.'

'Always handy for a cup of sugar,' said Lyn.

He turned to Helen. 'Bye, Helen and Rosie. I enjoyed meeting you both.'

Then he was gone.

'Are you looking forward to having him next door?' asked Jane.

Lyn had been thinking about this quite a lot, but was still not sure. 'Possibly,' she said. 'I'm sure he'll be all right. But I knew where I was with you. With him…?'

'Your life's going to change, isn't it?' Jane asked happily.

* * *

Next morning Lyn made a home visit to Annie Prince, a nineteen year old who was expecting her first baby in a couple of months. Annie had been coming regularly to antenatal classes, but Lyn always liked to see the home the baby would live in. Not that there would be any problem with Annie. Lyn had known her and her mother for years.

Annie and her husband Fred had a council house. Lyn looked at the front garden with approval. The perfect lawn and thickly flowered borders showed that Fred was a very keen gardener.

And the house was perfect, too. Annie, both elated and frightened, showed Lyn the newly decorated nursery with the new cot, blankets and baby clothes. And Annie's mum, living in the same village, was there to keep an eye on things. Lyn guessed that Annie was going to have plenty of support.

Time for a quick examination. Lyn did the usual obs and wrote them up. 'Nothing whatsoever to worry about,' she said. Then there was the equally necessary sit-down for a gossip.

'I heard that that new doctor has been on telly,' Annie said eagerly. 'In fact, I've seen him. He's ever so good-looking. And he's got a lovely voice. Can I sign on to have him, please?'

'Don't be so silly, Annie,' her mother said sharply. 'Dr Mitchell's been our doctor for years, and very good, too. You don't change something good just because you think you've seen something better on telly.'

Gently, Lyn said, 'I think they're both very good. Why not see what happens nearer the day?'

'That seems the best thing,' Annie's mother said.

But from behind her Lyn heard a mutinous Annie mutter, 'Other girls think that he's ever so good-looking, too.'

Lyn was back in the surgery at lunchtime and by chance happened to see Adam in the corridor. She ignored the sudden dart of excitement that flashed through her, caused by the sight of his broad shoulders, his happy smile. It was nothing really. They were colleagues, going to be friends. She was just not used to him yet. Or was there more to it?

'Your fame is spreading,' she said cheerfully. 'I've just had the second request to see you because you've been on TV.'

'But I've only just got here! How do people know?'

'Village bush telegraph. If one person knows something, then everyone does. You'll have to get used to that.'

'I suppose so.' He looked rather uncomfortable.

Lyn put her hand on his arm. 'Don't worry, we'll all protect you.'

Adam looked down at her hand, covered it with his own. 'I appreciate that.'

She was surprised at the effect that his touch had on her. It was almost as if they were holding hands, and his was warm and comforting. He looked at her and she wondered if those grey eyes were telling more than the open, friendly face.

Then a door opened behind them, the receptionist came out and his expression changed. It was hard to say how, it was still friendly, companion-like. But she was sure that there had been something more. But she wasn't sure what it was.

* * *

Jane finished moving that night. Lyn spent the evening with her, shifting the few last things, making decisions and cleaning. It wasn't a big house and wasn't dirty, but it was amazing what they found to do.

'If you stay in one place, you just acquire things,' Jane grumbled. 'I'm sure someone comes in and leaves things when you aren't looking. What am I doing with three half-used pots of marmalade, Lyn? Can I leave you a couple?'

'If you want. Aren't you going to leave anything for the new tenant?'

Jane considered. 'I don't think so. Cal says he's a good doctor, I liked what I saw of him last night, but I don't think we're on leaving half-empty marmalade pot terms yet. But you soon will be.'

'Well, we're all good friends in the practice,' Lyn said. 'We try to help each other. That's all there will be to it.'

'Of course,' said Jane.

The next day, as she was passing at lunchtime, Lyn saw men carrying boxes and furniture out of a furniture van into the empty cottage. The name on the side showed the van had come from London. Adam was moving in promptly, she thought. Of course, he wouldn't need much. The house was half-furnished already.

That evening she came home as usual, showered and changed into casual clothes. Then she took a deep breath, told herself that she was only being neighbourly and went next door. She found a perplexed Adam, sitting on the floor surrounded by boxes.

'I've come to be neighbourly,' she told him, 'or, if

you prefer the word, nosy. Can I do anything at all to help? Or would it be better if I just went back home and left you to suffer?'

'Stay, please, stay,' he said. 'Be neighbourly or nosy but, please, stay.' Together they looked at the piles of books, clothes, files and computer accessories. He pointed to the far wall. 'I've just cleared that wall and fixed up those bookshelves. How do you fancy filling them with these books?'

'Sounds a good idea. Any special system, order, organisation?'

He shrugged. 'I'm sure you'll work one out. And while you're doing that, I'll take these clothes upstairs then connect the computer.'

'We'll do an hour or so,' she said, 'then I'll go back next door, cook a quick meal and bring it round. Then we can finish the job.'

'That'll be great. Lyn, I've never had a neighbour like you.'

So they did as she'd suggested. After an hour she dashed back home and heated a beef stew she'd kept in her freezer and served it with fruit to follow. Then they worked again.

After a while she discovered that she wasn't just unpacking and putting away, she was helping Adam make decisions. Where were his pictures to hang, how to organise his kitchen, what to do with these three beautiful Persian rugs. She realised she was homemaking. She also realised that their tastes were very similar.

He had fitted two racks to hold his CDs, she opened a cardboard box labeled 'CDs' and looked through at the contents. 'You've got my favourite CDs here,' she shouted. 'I love them.'

'You fancy putting one on?'

'Great idea.' She reached over to switch on the CD player as he walked in. 'And before you unpack the rest of the discs, tell me what other music you like.'

After she'd listed her other favourite singers, she skimmed through the rest of his CDs, and gulped. Their tastes were uncannily alike—he had all the singers she had just mentioned. 'I didn't look,' she said. 'Honestly, I didn't look.'

'I know. We just like the same things. Nice, isn't it?'

It *was* nice but she decided to change the subject. 'What are you doing over there?' He was arranging something in an alcove and she couldn't quite see what.

'Come over and see.'

So she went. The alcove was lit from above, and in it he was hanging a selection of photographs, all in frames. They covered the top half of the alcove. 'Adam Fletcher, this is your life,' he said.

Lyn was fascinated, her eyes flitting from picture to picture. Some were obviously medical in origin—Adam with groups of other white-coated students. One of them showed him smiling broadly in cap and gown, holding his diploma over his head. Three or four pictures showed him with girls—all different, all attractive. She felt not jealous but interested. 'Any of your parents?' she asked.

Solemnly he pointed to a black-and-white photograph of a group of children. 'That's me,' he said, pointing to one. He was just recognisable, smiling, as he so often did, but looking cautious too.

'I was brought up in an orphanage,' he said. 'This

is St Mark's. Not the ideal way to bring up children, but I was loved and I was happy there.'

She felt for the first time a certain lack of confidence in him, as if he had just shown himself to be vulnerable. 'Is this why you so much want children of your own?'

He pondered. 'Possibly. But mostly I want children just because I like them. Now, are you going to pick a CD?'

He didn't want to talk any more about the orphanage or his upbringing. Well, that was fine. But she felt he had revealed something of himself, and she knew they'd talk more about it some other time.

By ten o'clock they had the house in some kind of order and decided to call it a day. 'I was very happy staying at the Red Lion,' he said, 'but if I had stayed much longer I would have weighed another three stone. It'll be good to have a place of my own. Now, as a small thank-you, may I take you down there and we can have a celebratory drink together?'

Her first reaction was to say no. She didn't go out for drinks with men. Then she thought, Why not? After all, they were neighbours. For a moment she considered inviting him into her house for coffee. But not just yet. Since Michael had died she'd never entertained a man in her house. But that wasn't exactly true. What she meant was that she had never entertained a man in her house she could be...interested in. Things were changing.

With a shock she realised that he was still waiting for her answer, a small smile on his face, almost as if he guessed what she had been thinking.

'Er, yes, why not?' she mumbled. 'I mean, that would be very nice. I'll just nip next door and change.

See you in ten minutes? We're sure to meet someone we know in the Red Lion.'

'So it won't be an intimate little get-together, just you and me?'

She laughed. 'You know the Red Lion. We'll be surrounded.'

She changed and they walked down to the village together. As she had known, as well as the tourists there were a fair number of locals there. She introduced Adam to Harry Sharpe, husband of Enid, the other district nurse. There were other people she knew, friends as well as patients. Adam bought her a glass of wine and had a beer himself. Then he sat in a corner with her and patiently answered questions about what it was like to appear on television.

'Do you mind all these questions?' she whispered to him when they had a minute to themselves.

He shook his head. 'People are entitled to be curious. And if they ask questions, it means I can ask questions, too. Just so long as they don't expect me to diagnose in the tap room.'

She laughed. 'It has been known to happen. But most people here have the right idea.'

'I never had a life like this in London. I was anonymous there. Here I feel I'm part of a community.'

'It can be constricting,' she warned. 'It's not always a good thing to have everyone knowing your business.'

'At least they care. London can be a lonely place.' Then they were joined again by Harry and had to talk about television again.

It was a glorious evening as they walked home. They paced up the lane leading to their cottages, and when they came out from the shadow of the great oak trees Adam looked up and said, 'See the stars. No smog here to hide them.'

'Beautiful,' she said curtly. She was feeling apprehensive, she didn't know how the evening was to end. Would he want to come in for coffee? She didn't want to have an intimate evening with a man. Well, certainly not yet. Though perhaps in the future things might be different. 'I'm feeling quite tired now,' she added.

'I'm not surprised. You've had a hard day at work and then spent the evening helping me. You're entitled to be tired.'

Lyn could hear the amusement in his voice. He had guessed what was worrying her. Well too bad.

Soon they were at her own front door and to her irritation she felt herself tensing. Almost in desperation she decided to act so that things would go the way she wanted them to. Quickly she took his arm, reached up and kissed him on the cheek. Then she stepped firmly backwards, out of his reach. 'I've had a lovely evening,' she gabbled. 'Welcome to your new home and I hope we'll be happy neighbours.'

Again there was amusement in his voice. 'I'm sure we'll be very happy living…next to each other.' She was sure that the pause had been deliberate. He went on, 'There's no hurry about anything, is there, Lyn? We're getting to know each other.'

'No hurry about anything at all. Goodnight, Adam.' And then she was in her own house, leaning against the closed front door, wondering why she was trembling.

She undressed, put on her nightgown and sat in her living room with her usual mug of cocoa. As she so often did, she gazed at the photograph of her dead husband. It was now three years since the accident. Slowly he was turning into a memory, not a constant part of her life. She still loved him, but she realised that that love wasn't the open wound on her soul that it had once been. Her life was moving on.

Lyn's work took her into Keldale the next afternoon. She passed an art shop with a display of pen-and-ink drawings of the Lake District. On impulse she went inside, browsed for a while and then bought two. One she wanted for her own bedroom. The other she thought would do as a house-warming present for Adam. She wrote a short note on the back of Adam's picture and then had it properly wrapped.

When she got back to her cottage the next evening there was a note pushed through her letter-box.

'Dr Adam Fletcher, now at home at number two Dale End Cottages, requests the pleasure of the company of Mrs Lyn Pierce this evening for drinks at eight. (Actually, a glass of sherry.) No need to RSVP. Come if you can.'

Lyn smiled and sat down to write a reply. 'Mrs Lyn Pierce thanks Dr Adam Fletcher for his kind invitation to drinks and takes great pleasure in accepting. And I *always* RSVP.' Then she ran next door and pushed the note through his letter-box. She was rather looking forward to the evening.

At seven she ran herself a bath and then searched through her wardrobe for a summer dress, something just a bit showy. She had plenty of dresses, but she didn't wear them very often any more. After some thought she decided on a sleeveless dress in a deep yellow shade. She thought it went well with her hair.

At exactly eight o'clock she knocked on his door.

She carried the house-warming present she had bought him, and she could feel her heart beating faster than usual. Well, she had been in a bit of a hurry in the last five minutes.

But when she saw him her heart actually lurched. It was as if she hadn't seen him for a month, instead of just twenty-four hours. He looked so new, so good!

He was dressed in a soft white shirt and light grey trousers. And he was smiling at her as if she was the one person in the world he most wanted to see.

'Lyn, come in, how nice to see you! The first guest in my new home. Last night you did most of the hard work, and today I've just cleaned round a little and thrown the rubbish away. I know I'm going to be happy here...next to you.'

She followed him into the living room, the same room where she'd worked the night before, but now it was like a home, not a workplace. All the packing had been cleared away, there were flowers in vases, the chairs were better organised. This wasn't the room where she'd sat so often with Jane. It was a man's room.

Shyly, she offered him his house-warming present. 'This is to welcome you to Keldale. I hope you'll be happy here.'

'A present! I love presents!' He tore off the wrapping. 'Lyn, this is beautiful. Look, it'll hang here, just over the mantelpiece. There's no time like now.'

Then he turned to the back. 'Be happy in your new home,' he read, 'Love, Lyn.' He looked at her and she couldn't read his expression. 'Love, Lyn,' he said. 'That's nice. I know I'm going to be happy here, the more so because I'm living next door to you.'

'It's only a picture. I bought myself one just like it.'

'Did you?' he asked. 'Isn't it good that we seem to like the same things?'

Then, before she realized what he was doing, he'd fetched a hammer and a hook, and had hung the picture on the wall. The picture looked really good. She could tell his enthusiasm was genuine.

'That is great, thank you so much,' he said, and kissed her on the cheek. 'Now, would you like a sherry? And being traditional, I've bought some fruit cake to go with it.'

So they drank a glass of sherry and had a slice of fruit cake, and she decided this was a very civilised way of spending half an hour. She sat in one of his comfortable armchairs and felt very much at ease.

'You seem to be fitting in well here,' she said.

'I hope so. I was a bit worried at first, I wondered if country people might be suspicious of newcomers, might be slow to accept me. But I've met with nothing but kindness.'

'We try to make people welcome,' she said softly. 'We want to be friendly.'

'I know that's true.' Adam looked at her, thoughtfully, almost assessingly. 'Being friendly,' he said, 'if you're not going sailing again or doing anything similar, would you like to spend next Saturday afternoon and evening with me?'

'Spend time with you? Doing what?'

'I'd really like it to be a surprise. Nothing heavy, but something that would show you a little about me.'

Her first reaction was to say yes because she rather fancied the idea. But then she thought some more and her native caution advised her against it. 'I'd like to spend the time with you,' she said slowly. 'I'd really like to, and I'm not going sailing. But I'm going to say no.'

He said nothing, just looked at her, his expression sympathetic, alert. She knew she had to go on. 'I don't want to seem forward or anything,' she faltered, 'but I think we might be getting...too close to each other. And I'm scared. Perhaps we should remain friends or even just acquaintances. That might be better for us. Well, it might be better for me. I'm sorry, Adam, perhaps I'm making too much over what is just a simple invitation, but I really am frightened.'

'I wouldn't want to frighten you, Lyn, not for anything. And you must decide what's best for you. But can you tell me why you're frightened?' Such a calm, understanding voice!

For a moment she thought she would smile, shake her head, finish her drink and leave without saying anything. She knew he would accept that. But then she decided she wanted him to understand. He was owed an explanation.

'You know I was married. I loved Michael in a way I didn't think it possible to love anyone. They say that after a few years love becomes quieter, gentler, turns into something like a habit. Well, with us it didn't. I was as much in love with him after five years as I was the day I married him.'

Now Lyn knew her voice was trembling. 'We were going to have a baby and I was so much looking forward to it, and I lost it. Not an it, it was a little girl! But we still had each other and we had a future together. Then, one perfectly ordinary day, he went out in the morning, and in the afternoon I was told he'd been killed. It tore the heart out of me.'

The tears were running down her face now. But she had to go on, to explain. Adam was owed that. 'Perhaps I've got over the worst of it, but I decided afterwards that I would never risk being in love again. The pain was too great, the heartache too much. I've had men want to take me out, ask me to dinner and so on, but I've never said yes. It just isn't worth the risk.'

She saw him half stand, as if to come over to her, then, quite deliberately, he sat down again. She liked him for that. He would wait a while till she was calmer.

After a moment she went to his bathroom, washed her face in cold water. when she felt a little better she returned and said, 'I'm sorry about that. I usually keep my feelings well under control.'

'People are meant to have feelings. If you control them too well you lose something very valuable.'

He paused for a moment then went on, 'I sympathise with you, I really do. And I think anyone who has had a love such as you described is to be envied. But I think that I want something from you and I'm going to ask you for it.'

She could tell he was choosing his words with care, making sure that he said exactly what he meant. There must be no margin for error. 'I'm not sure about this, neither of us is sure. But I think you've felt something for me, right from the time when you first opened your eyes on the boat. I felt a spark then, like nothing I'd felt before.'

She had to be honest. 'Yes. I did feel it.'

'Lyn if you want nothing more to do with me, then you must tell me. You must say so face to face. I'm not going to be awkward with you, but I think I'm entitled to hear you say it.'

She was silent. Did she want to tell him she wanted nothing more to do with him? Could she say it? She knew he'd accept her decision, no matter how reluctantly.

'May I have another sherry, please?' she asked at last.

Wordlessly, he filled her glass.

'I can't say I don't want to go out with you. And I'd like to go out with you on Saturday. But it commits me to nothing. This is an afternoon out, two friends together. Afterwards we might see more of each other...or not.'

'That's fine,' he said quietly. 'I'm glad you're coming with me.'

Lyn searched his face for any sign of triumph. There was none there—just pleasure. And now she found she was more relaxed. More than relaxed, she was intrigued, and she was quite looking forward to an afternoon with someone. It struck her that her social life was rather solitary. Most of her time—as in the boat—she spent alone.

'I quite like secrets, but you must give me some hint,' she said. 'What do I wear? Climbing boots or party dress?'

Adam looked perplexed. 'That's quite a good question, and I hadn't thought about it. Put it this way, I'll be wearing trousers and a casual shirt with a pair of reasonably stout shoes. And carrying a waterproof, 'cos this is England.'

'I get the picture.' She smiled. 'I can do that.'

Lyn finished her second glass of sherry. 'I've only

had two drinks,' she said, 'but I can feel they've had an effect on me. I think I'd better go.'

'I'm so glad you came,' Adam murmured softly, 'I think we're getting somewhere. But there's no hurry.'

She went home and sat and thought about what had just happened, the decision she had just made. By agreeing to go out with him she had made herself vulnerable—something she had sworn never to do again. But she found she didn't mind.

Adam had said to her that if you controlled feelings too well you lost something very valuable. That was an interesting thought. Her life over the past years now seemed a little flat. Perhaps she could risk something.

She took the picture of Michael from its place on the mantelpiece and sat with it on her lap. She studied it, as she had done a thousand times before. What would Michael advise her to do now?

She knew above all that he would want her to be happy. And she thought she could read an answer in that much-loved face. She should go for happiness—even if it meant taking a risk.

CHAPTER FOUR

Days later Cal and Adam got out of Cal's car and looked at the village of Tyndale below them. There was the church, houses and cottages, a scattering of farm buildings, all in a green hollow in the hills.

'It seems a picture-postcard kind of place,' Adam said.

Cal nodded. 'It is. But it's miles from the nearest town and miles from the surgery. After privatisation they cut the bus service, and it only calls three times a week now.'

'So if someone needs medical attention and they haven't got a car...?'

'They're in trouble,' Cal said.

Both Cal and Adam had been busy, and this was the first time they had been able to get together. After morning surgery Cal invited Adam to drive out with him. 'Get to know a bit of the countryside,' he had said. And they finished up at Tyndale. Adam wondered exactly what Cal had in mind. He knew this wasn't just a casual invitation.

They got back into Cal's car and drove down the steep slope into the village. They parked by a village hall next to the church where, waiting for them, there was a beaming vicar. 'The Reverend Peter McCarthy.' Cal introduced them. 'He's got an idea for us.'

Rev. McCarthy said he was pleased to see them, that they should call him Peter and should they get on at once? He led them into the village hall. It was a clean, well-decorated place, obviously lovingly maintained. They walked past the stacked chairs, the piano, the display by the local Guides and Scouts.

'Kitchen,' Peter pointed out. 'A fridge-freezer, three stoves. A good boiler, there's plenty of hot water and in winter this place is the warmest in the village. Toilets for men and women, both newly installed. And down there there's a shower and bathroom.'

He unlocked two further doors, showed them small empty rooms, each with a sink in the corner. 'And these were what I had in mind for you.'

Adam turned to Cal, lifted his eyebrows. 'Peter wants us to hold a branch surgery here,' Cal said. 'Have a doctor and nurse in attendance perhaps one morning a week. In principle I'm very much in favour of the idea. But I brought you along to look for problems, to act as devil's advocate. Tell me what you think.'

Peter offered Adam a list of names. 'These are all local people who are members of your practice. A lot of them are old, a lot of them are not very well off. A surgery they could walk to would be of vast benefit.' He looked at Adam expectantly.

Adam walked round the rooms, turned on the taps, peered into the toilets, the bathroom, the kitchen. 'I think it's a great idea,' he said eventually.

'How would you like to set it up, get it running?' Cal asked.

'Nothing would please me more.'

Half an hour later Cal and Adam were enjoying a beef sandwich at the local pub. As Cal said, they had to get a feel for the area. 'There's government money available for branch surgeries,' he said. 'We'll let the practice manager do the applying, though. You'd better give her a list of the equipment you'll need.'

Adam nodded. 'I don't want to set up a complete surgery,' he said. 'I see this is a first line of defence. I suspect we'll have to organise transport for quite a few to come to us in Keldale.'

'True. But they'll be in the system. That must be good.'

'I'm looking forward to starting it.'

Cal took an enjoyable mouthful of sandwich. 'So you're happy here? Things aren't too quiet for you after the big city?'

'Quiet! I haven't had a dull day yet. And people here are so friendly I feel like I've joined a family.'

'Quite so. You've fitted in well here. Getting on all right with Lyn, your next-door neighbour?'

Adam realised that the question wasn't as casual as it had sounded. 'I think Lyn is wonderful,' he said. 'I've never met a woman like her.'

Cal grinned. 'I take it that isn't a reflection on her abilities as a midwife?'

'Not entirely, no. Are you worried that I might...upset her in any way?'

Cal thought about this. 'Lyn is a close friend. I knew her husband and I've seen how she's suffered since he died. I wouldn't want anyone to hurt her, she's still vulnerable. But...I've got Jane now and I think everyone should be as happy as we two are.'

'I'd like to make Lyn happy,' Adam said.

That morning she woke feeling unusually cheerful. There had been no special reason. It had been a wonderful morning but, then, the weather had been fine for weeks. She'd just felt cheerful. Life was good.

She'd wondered about her mood as she'd washed, dressed and sat in a sunny corner of the kitchen to eat her breakfast. Yesterday she had made a decision, which was out of her hands now. She had agreed to go out with Adam. Where was he going to take her, would it make a difference to the way she felt about him? Would it make a difference to the way she felt about herself? It was in the lap of the gods now.

The cottages were very stoutly built, it was seldom that she heard anything from next door. Occasionally there would be sound of music, or a knock or a rattle, and she'd be aware that he was close to her, only a few feet separating them. It was an oddly exciting thought.

She set off on her rounds, and on impulse decided to call on Julie Harris. There was no real need—had there been any problems Julie would have phoned. But she hadn't seen her since her weekend away. It would be nice to see if it had gone well.

When she arrived it was easy to see that Julie was much happier. The dark marks under her eyes had gone, she looked more relaxed, had a bigger smile.

'Come and look at the baby first then I'll put the kettle on and you can see the snaps we took at the weekend. Lyn, we had a fantastic time!'

'I'm glad you enjoyed yourselves.'

'You wouldn't believe it.'

So Lyn looked at pictures of the Minster, of Julie and Bill on the ramparts, of Julie and Bill rowing on the river. They did look happy. Lyn felt almost jealous of the pleasure she could see the two felt in each other's company.

'It was really good to get away, Lyn. Me and Bill had time for each other. He thought it was wonderful, too.' Julie coloured slightly. 'Things between us were so much better when we had plenty of time, and we weren't worried about the baby crying. It quite perked us both up.'

'Good,' said Lyn, wondering if Julie would be needing her professional services in nine months' time. 'So Bill's parents were happy enough, baby-sitting?'

'They enjoyed it, too, said they'd do it again whenever we liked.'

'So next time will be?' Lyn probed.

Julie shrugged. 'Some time. In a few months. It's funny. Like I said, we both enjoyed getting away, but I was looking forward to getting back again to my baby.'

She leaned over, peered down into the cot. 'You know, I used to be always off having a good time. But now I'm happy staying at home. Being a mother completely changes the way you see things.'

Julie sipped her tea. 'Have you never wanted kids, Lyn? It seems a bit strange, being a midwife, an expert and all, and not having children yourself.'

The question had only been asked casually, but Lyn had to strive to answer back equally casually. 'Some day perhaps. When I find Mr Right. At the moment I get a big enough kick out of other people's babies.'

Lyn had to call home before going out that afternoon. As she ate her light lunch she thought of Julie's question and her own answer. 'When I find Mr Right.'

Three and a half years ago she'd had a miscarriage. She had haemorrhaged and had been taken urgently to the local hospital, then moved to a large O and G unit in Leeds. Mr Smilie, her consultant, had diagnosed pelvic inflammatory disease. Hers had been one of those rarest of cases—it had just happened, there had been no obvious cause. When he'd discharged her Mr Smilie had told her that she wasn't to attempt to have another child for at least a year. But then, six months later, Michael had been killed.

She still saw Mr. Smilie once a year and they had become friends. 'Just a little precaution, my dear,' he had said, 'just to check up on how you are getting on. After all, we professionals have to stick together.'

She sat motionless for fifteen minutes, not noticing that the mug of tea in her hand was growing cold. Then, slowly, she reached for her phone.

Mr Smilie's secretary remembered her, and because there'd been a cancellation could fit her in the following Friday. 'Just an ordinary check, is it?' she asked. 'No signs of anything wrong, no cause for worry?'

It took Lyn a while to answer. 'I just wondered,' she said. 'There's no great worry but I just wondered...could Mr Smilie tell me if it would be all right for me to...that is, could I...? I want to know if I could conceive.'

'I'll make a note of that,' said the secretary.

Lyn picked up her mug of tea, sipped and then winced when she found it stone cold. Why had she asked that? What did it matter to her anyway? A part of her mind knew the answer to the question but she refused to face up to it. She would progress a little at a time.

She had no set clinics on Friday so it was easy to book a day's holiday. She was up early. If she had to go, then she would enjoy it.

Driving to Leeds was easy. She parked near the centre and had a happy couple of hours walking round the shops. After an early lunch she drove to the outskirts of the city and parked in the hospital grounds. Her appointment was for one forty-five. She was early but Mr Smilie was ready for her.

'Ah, Midwife Pierce! Another one bringing babies into the world. Now, how have you been?'

She like Mr Smilie. She was comfortable with the kindly man and he treated her like a daughter. Vaguely she wondered how old he was, deciding he must be nearing sixty-five, when all National Health consultants had to retire.

Quickly he went through the usual examination. It was what she was used to, largely what, indeed, she gave to her own mums. As she'd expected, there was no change in anything. But this time she wasn't to smile, shake hands and leave. She had asked for a further examination, for an answer to a specific question. 'I gather you have more to ask me, Lyn?' Mr Smilie said calmly.

She still hesitated. Just to ask the question meant making a commitment to herself, meant she was thinking about things that until recently had been forbidden. It was a question that would open doors she had kept firmly closed.

'Mr Smilie, when I first came to see you over three years ago, you told me not to try to have children for at least a year and then to come and see you again. After that my...my husband was killed and it didn't really matter. But what if...? Could I have children now?'

She had asked him and now there was no going

back. Later she would have to ask herself again—why did she want to know? She couldn't pretend that it was just curiosity.

He looked at her thoughtfully. 'I take it that there's a reason for the question.' Then a smile spread across his face. 'Are you thinking of getting married again? You've met a good man?'

She couldn't give him an honest answer. She didn't know the answer to that question herself. So she said hurriedly, 'No, I'm not thinking of getting married. But who knows what the future might bring? I'd just like to know.'

Mr Smilie nodded and flipped through her notes. 'Well, there was a fair amount of scarring. Just how competent are your Fallopian tubes...your cervix...I don't know.' He frowned, the smiled. 'I've arranged to send you for the usual battery of tests—bloods, ultrasound, X-ray. I can't tell from the examination I've just conducted. You obviously want to know quickly so we'll cut a few corners. It would be a pity if we baby-bringers couldn't help each other.'

He took a set of forms from his desk, started to scribble on them. 'You're jumping the queue so you're going to have a busy time. You can have all the tests this afternoon and I'll write to you in a few days when I've reviewed the results.'

Lyn was silent. What had she started?

All the way through the journey back to Keldale the question kept hammering at her. Why had she asked if she could have babies? Was it just idle curiosity? She couldn't or wouldn't give herself an answer. Obviously it was something to do with Adam Fletcher. But further than that she would not go.

* * *

Now Lyn was actively looking forward to spending Saturday with Adam—and also very curious. She met him in the corridor at the surgery a couple of times and asked him again where they were going. He wouldn't tell. 'Surprises are always fun,' he told her with a grin. 'I want to surprise you. And whatever you wear will be fine.'

Saturday was another really fine day. Lyn spent quite a lot of time thinking, then dressed in light trousers with a pink blouse and a grey leather jacket. Casual, but smart, too. It seemed to cover every eventuality.

They'd agreed that they would set off at eleven. She heard Adam leave at nine o' clock and come back an hour later. Then he knocked on her door at eleven and they were off.

He was dressed equally casually, in dark grey trousers and a dark blue shirt. Whatever they were to do, they were dressed alike.

Like most of the others in the practice, he had bought a four-wheel drive vehicle. She noticed that in the back of it there were two large cardboard boxes. 'What type of trip are we going on?' she asked. 'What's in those boxes?'

'All will be revealed. You're going to see what I do best—and like most.' More than that he wouldn't say.

They drove past Keldale onto the motorway and headed south. After a while he turned off, threaded his way through obviously well-known back roads and emerged somewhere on the outskirts of Lancaster. Then, in a pleasant, older suburb, he turned into the drive of a semi, stopped and beeped his horn.

Only then did he turn to her, and she thought she could see doubt and hope in his expression.

'Hope you're going to enjoy yourself,' he said. 'This might not be what you were expecting.'

Down the drive ran a boy and a girl, Lyn guessed the boy to be aged about seven, the girl nine. 'Uncle Adam, Uncle Adam,' they both shouted, obviously excited to see him. He opened the car door and the girl kissed him, but the boy didn't.

Adam turned to Lyn with a rueful expression. 'My nephew John and my niece Bella. I told you we'd come to do what I like most. I've brought you to meet the only family I have.'

Now a smiling, attractive woman, slightly older than Adam, came down the drive. She hugged and kissed him, held onto his hand. 'Adam, it's so good to see you!' Then she turned questioningly to Lyn, who had just got out of the car. 'And you must be Lyn.'

'My sister Emma,' said Adam. 'We're very close. We've been through a lot together.'

Lyn saw the way they looked at each other, stood close together. 'I can believe it,' she said.

Emma shook her hand, then leaned forward and hugged her. 'He's a terrible man, my brother,' she said. 'He's told me a lot about you and I've been wanting to meet you.' She stood back and surveyed Lyn. 'He said you were lovely.'

Lyn blushed. 'He didn't tell me about you,' she said.

'Well, that's good. Now, d'you want to come inside for a minute because I gather we're—?'

'Uncle Adam, Uncle Adam, where's our picnic? You said you would take us on a picnic!'

'It's in the back, monsters! But nothing to eat till we get to the seaside. We have to have a run on the sands first.'

'Give Uncle Adam a chance,' Emma said, 'and come and say hello to Auntie Lyn.' Dutifully the two children shook hands. Lyn was aware of being scrutinised.

'Uncle Adam's never brought a lady before,' Bella said.

'Inside, you two,' said Emma briskly. 'We'll set off on the picnic in ten minutes.'

They were shown into a pleasant living room where a picture of a smiling bearded man caught Lyn's attention.

'That's my daddy,' Bella said, seeing Lyn looking at the picture.

'My husband Ben,' Emma said. 'He's away on an oil rig at the moment but we're going to see him again in a couple of weeks.'

Lyn couldn't help asking. 'Is he away much?'

'He's away a lot and we miss him. But it's a life he loves, though he loves us, too. And it's wonderful when he does come home. So we manage. And now that Adam's so close that we see a lot of him, I hope he doesn't go back to London.'

'He seems to be very happy in Keldale,' Lyn said, 'and he's a good doctor.' She wasn't sure what else to say.

At the children's insistence they decided not to have a drink but to set off for the seaside at once. Adam drove through Lancaster, along a canal and then to a village where there were miles of golden sands. They parked easily, and Emma and Lyn unpacked onto a handy picnic table while Adam rolled up his trousers and took John and Bella for a run and a paddle.

'I gather you live next to Adam,' Emma said casually. 'He's lucky to find somewhere so close to his place of work.'

'They're nice little cottages,' Lyn admitted, 'but I would have thought he'd find them a bit...well, simple after apparently living in a luxury flat in London.'

'You've not been to his flat?'

'No. We haven't really known each other for very long. I don't think I'm on visiting-his-London-flat terms.'

'You will be,' Emma said cheerfully, 'or, at least, I hope you will be. The London flat is great for a weekend or four or five days. I've often been with the kids, but I wouldn't want to live there. A rackety sort of life he leads. He's better off up here.'

The children then came back, puffing and panting, saying that they'd run for miles and that they'd seen little crabs in the water and some seaweed and fishing boats, and wasn't it time for the picnic now? Emma rubbed dirty hands with a roll of wipes and then the five of them sat to eat. There was a Thermos of coffee for the adults and soft drinks for the children. And the picnic was marvellous. Lyn knew the firm that had packed it. They were usually very good but this time they'd excelled themselves.

'What d'you do, Auntie Lyn?' Bella asked after a while.

'I'm a midwife. I help ladies have babies.'

'Uncle Adam is a doctor, he helps people when they're sick. Is it like that?'

'Yes, but having a baby isn't the same as being

sick. Most people I work with really like having a baby.'

'But doesn't it hurt? I saw this film on telly when Mummy was out of the room and this lady having a baby was shouting ever so loudly.' Bella was wide-eyed.

'Well, yes, it can hurt,' Lyn allowed, 'but it's over quite quickly and we have drugs and things to make it easier. People are happy about it afterwards.'

She saw Emma's smiling face. Emma winked. 'That's what my midwife said. I was happy about it afterwards, but at the time I wasn't so sure.'

After they had finished the picnic they packed what remained into the cardboard boxes and went together for another walk. But it had been a long warm day in the open air and after a while the children started to flag. 'Time to get two little ones bathed and in front of the television,' Adam said. 'What d'you want to watch tonight Bella?'

'I read mostly now,' Bella said with dignity. 'Television is for children.'

'Sorry,' murmured Adam, somehow keeping his face straight.

Lyn had enjoyed herself, she'd had a gentle relaxing day. It had been completely the opposite of what she had been half expecting—and because of that it had been more pleasant.

They drove back to Emma's house, had a quick cup of tea and then Adam said they had better be going. 'We will see you again quite soon, won't we, Lyn?' Emma asked. 'If you can't persuade this cantankerous old man to bring you, then come on your own.'

'I'll certainly come,' said Lyn. 'And he's not very cantankerous.'

Bella kissed her goodbye and, after a bit of pushing, John did the same. Emma gave her a hard hug and whispered, 'You make sure he brings you.' And then they were gone.

Lyn hadn't had a chance for any time alone with Adam and he was surprisingly anxious. 'Did you enjoy yourself?' he asked. 'You weren't a bit disappointed?'

'How can you ask that? I had a lovely time. But I was surprised. I half expected some supposedly classy experience, with you trying to impress me. This was so much nicer. But why did you want to take me there so much?'

He paused. 'I wanted you to see what I think is the real me. See me as I am. As you said, I could have taken you to some classy place, some glamorous TV experience. But I didn't want to. Are you disappointed?'

'You know I'm not.' She reached over and rubbed the side of his arm. 'I like the real you.'

For a moment Lyn was quiet as it was difficult for Adam to negotiate his way onto the motorway. But when they were travelling steadily she went on, 'You're very close to your sister, aren't you?'

'Very close. I love her and, what is great, I get on very well with her husband. It's a pity he has to be away so much, but otherwise they're the kind of family that I want to be part of.'

'Yes,' she said thoughtfully. 'Were you in the orphanage together?'

'We were. She's a few of years older than me, perhaps she suffered more at first. But we managed to look after each other.'

It was only early evening when they got back. This time Lyn didn't hesitate. 'Would you like to come in and have tea with me? Don't expect much after that picnic, but I could do something on toast.'

'I'd love to. But I'm a bit sandy. Shall I go and have a bath first and come round in twenty minutes?'

'Good idea. I'll have a bath.'

First she selected a dress to put on, another one she hadn't worn for quite some time, this time in dark green. Then she had her bath and sat in fresh, dainty underwear in front of her dressing-table mirror. The day out in the sun had put extra colour in her cheeks, she knew she looked well. There was a sparkle in her eyes, a feeling of excitement pulsing through her. She was looking forward to her evening.

Adam arrived five minutes later. He had also changed, into a white shirt and dark trousers. 'You look good in green,' he said. 'It goes well with your eyes.'

'Thank you. Now, come straight into the kitchen, I've created a real feast. We're having boiled eggs and salad with fruit to follow.'

'If it's with you, it will be a feast,' he said.

In fact, the meal wasn't at all bad. The eggs came from a farm she visited, and were fresh and genuinely free range. The bread was from a local baker. 'You're going to have to give me a set of addresses,' he said when she told him this. 'There's more to this country living business than I realised.'

Afterwards they took their teacups into the living room. He looked round curiously, saw the picture on the corner of the mantelpiece. He reached for it. 'Your husband? May I?' he asked.

She nodded. He took up the picture, turned it to the light. 'He looks a kind man.'

'He was. I knew Michael since we were in primary school together. We always knew we were going to get married and when we did we were as happy as we'd expected. And he died. I'll always love him.'

He looked at the picture a little longer. 'That's fine, Lyn. But the past shouldn't be allowed to shadow the future completely. It's wrong to let it do that.'

She didn't like that and snatched the picture from him. 'You don't know what you're talking about! You've never been married. How can you know what it's like to lose someone who's the centre of your life?'

There was silence for a moment. Then she looked at his hunched figure, his bleak face. There was a message there. In spite of her anger she said, 'You do know what you're talking about, don't you?'

He shrugged. 'Possibly. Who can tell?'

Now she could see that he was forcing himself to be calm. He sat in the easy chair behind him, deliberately stretched out his legs and made himself relax.

'My parents died when I was very young, but I can just remember them. Emma is a few years older, she can remember them better. However, I remember them. I was settled enough in the orphanage but... believe it or not, I found that I hated my parents. They had died and left me. How could they?'

He was quiet for a moment, then went on, 'But I learned to forgive them and it made me feel better. I had a life to lead.'

'You're telling me this for a reason, aren't you?'

she demanded. 'You think this applies to Michael and me. Well, it doesn't!'

He shook his head. 'People are all different. I'm only telling you that I felt happier when I could let go. And it certainly took some time.'

Now they were both silent. 'I'm sorry I shouted at you,' she said after a while. 'I know you were only thinking of me.'

He nodded. 'I think of you quite a lot. It's been a full day. Perhaps I ought to go now.'

She went with him to the door. She could have asked him to stay, but he was right. They both needed time to think. At the door she took hold of him, pulled him to her and kissed him. She wanted to show him that she was her own woman. And although she was nervous she knew how much she wanted to kiss him.

He sensed her fear. At first he held her as if she were a tiny bird in the palm of his hand. But as she leaned against him their kiss became even more passionate. Thoughts, feelings she hadn't experienced in years tumbled through her mind. He was the first to break off their kiss. 'I've had a wonderful day,' he murmured. Then he kissed her once more on the cheek and was gone.

My life is changing, Lyn thought to herself. Then she thought again and decided, No...my life has changed.

The next evening Lyn walked over to Cal's house and sat with Jane in the garden. She and Jane drank iced lemonade as Cal worked. He said he needed the exercise.

Helen sat dozing on Jane's lap as Lyn confided in

her friend. 'I think I'm finally getting over Michael's death,' she said. 'I'm coming into the world again.'

'If you're ready. Don't let me or anyone push you, but personally I think you are ready. Has the appearance of a handsome young doctor anything to do with it?'

'Hmm. Possibly yes. I'm getting…very fond of Adam and it's surprised me that it's happened so quickly. And I suppose it's scared me a bit, too. Look at him. Every young girl's ideal. He could have anyone he wanted. Why pick on me?'

''Cos you're gorgeous,' Jane said cheerfully. 'So I gather things are going well between you?'

'Pretty well. I don't know though, I'm a quiet woman and I like quiet things. I certainly don't want to go to London—but Adam seems to prefer it up here. For the past three years I've been reasonably, well, contented. I don't want more heartache.'

Jane pondered. 'You know what?' she said. 'You need to step out. Why not go into town next weekend and buy some new clothes?'

'But I don't need any! Where would I go in new clothes?'

'You buy some new clothes and your chance will come. Take my word for it.'

CHAPTER FIVE

ADAM was realising that the idea of a branch surgery was a good one. He had also realised what a treasure the practice had in Eunice Padgett, the practice manager. Eunice had dealt with insurance, supply of equipment, hire of the premises. She had organised a mail-shot of all those in Tyndale who might be interested. She had liaised with Peter McCarthy and had found him a man after her own heart. And now Adam had just finished his first session at the branch. It had been a useful day.

'Like you said, we're going to get the old and the not well off first of all,' he said to Cal later as they talked in the coffee-room that afternoon. 'A couple of the older ones either couldn't get into Keldale or couldn't be bothered trying. I found one lady with a very suspicious chest—I've arranged for an ambulance to pick her up and take her to hospital for tests. And there's another thing...'

'Come on,' said Cal, 'I'm more interested in your doubts than your certainties.'

'Harry Kerr. Farmworker, aged forty-eight, apparently lives with his wife and three children in a tied cottage. Says he can't afford to be ill, whatever that means. I've looked at his notes and so far he's been very healthy. He presented with a very unpleasant cough and a skin rash, said he'd had both for weeks. He's been feeling bad all the time but he daren't take time off work, said he's needed. He just wanted a tonic.'

'A tonic,' said Cal. 'A little bottle of pink medicine to make him all right?'

'That kind of thing. I tried to get him to talk about his work and I wondered...I wondered about organophosphate poisoning. He told me he'd been handling some new kind of weedkiller and, yes, some did spill, it always does. Frankly, it's something I've never come across before.'

Cal scowled. 'You could well be right. Most of the local farmers are very careful, but one or two... What did you tell Harry?'

'I took a blood sample and told him we'd let him know. But probably I'd like to see him next week.'

'Sounds good. Let's get that sample to the lab. So, you had a good day?'

'It was satisfying,' replied Adam. 'And I made a lot of new friends.'

Even though they were next-door neighbours she didn't see Adam for a couple of days. There were a number of calls on her time, and she knew he, too, was being kept busy. In one way she didn't mind not seeing him. She had so much to think about, new ideas to get used to, so a breathing space was quite a good idea.

She decided to have a domestic evening and did some baking. When she had time she found that baking was soothing, therapeutic. So she fetched out her packets of dried fruit, nuts and so on and baked three super-rich cakes. And they were good! After trying a slice she wrapped one in a cloth, put it in a tin and left it on his doorstep with a little note. 'Felt domesticated, Made you a cake. Lyn.'

Next morning the tin was back on her own doorstep, filled with flowers and with a note back. 'Wonderful cake! I'm having to ration myself. Midwife, sailor, house organiser and now baker. Can't wait to find out what other talents you have. Adam.'

She smiled, and put the flowers in a vase. Things were progressing.

Next evening she was home in good time and decided to call on him later when she knew he'd be back from evening surgery. A call just for a chat and a cup of tea. See how he was settling in. Be a good neighbour.

She was surprised when she heard a car engine stop outside and went to look through the window. Not many cars stopped here. The car was actually outside Adam's house, a new, highly polished, dark green Jaguar. Not at all a local kind of car.

The Jaguar wasn't very well parked. As Lyn watched, a woman climbed out of the driver's seat, rather unsteadily, Lyn thought. She staggered, had to hold onto the car.

The woman was slim, very well dressed, in light-coloured leather trousers, high heels and what seemed to be a blue silk blouse. She was blonde, with big hair, an obviously professionally styled confection of curls. Lyn guessed her to be about forty.

The woman went to Adam's door, leaned against it and knocked. Of course, there was no answer. And when she tried to knock again Lyn saw that there was a scarf wrapped round one hand, and it appeared to be bloodstained.

Lyn did the neighbourly thing, and went to talk to

the woman. 'Do you want Dr Fletcher? I'm sorry, he's at evening surgery and will be for the next hour or so.'

The woman swayed slightly. 'Typical Adam. When you want him urgently he's somewhere else.'

'I'm Lyn Pierce. I'm a midwife at the practice and a friend of Adam's. May I help in any way?'

The woman smiled, then grimaced with pain. 'I'm Ros Roswell, I'm Adam's TV producer. I did hope for a bit of professional skill from him. Stupid of me, I got out my map to check the route, tripped over my own heels and fell against a post. I gashed my hand, I think it was on some barbed wire, and since he's supposed to be a doctor and...'

Lyn realised that the woman was in shock, didn't really know what she was saying. She interrupted. 'I'm a nurse as well as a midwife. Come and sit down in my house, take it easy for a while, and I'll bathe and dress your hand. You've had a shock.'

'But I've got to see Adam and—'

'When he comes home he'll see your car and call in here. Now, come and sit down before you fall down.' Lyn put out a hand to steady the woman.

'Yes, I'd think I need to sit down.' The woman glanced at Lyn's hand, saw the ring. 'It's very good of you Mrs...Mrs...'

'Mrs Pierce. But call me Lyn.' Lyn helped the woman through her front door. She wasn't going to explain to the woman that she was a widow. There was no time now.

She sat Ros in an easy chair, had a quick look at the cut. It was very long but not too deep. Obviously it was painful, cuts on the hands always were. Lyn decided she'd wait a minute before dressing it.

She fetched Ros the traditional cup of over-sweet tea, told her that perhaps it wasn't very nice but it was to push up her blood-sugar level. She also gave her a couple of painkillers. And after a while the colour came back to Ros's cheeks.

Then Lyn fetched her own medical kit, cleaned the cut and closed it with butterfly stitches. 'I don't think you need this sutured,' she said. 'I've done my time in A and E and these should be good enough. But we can ask Adam to take a look when he comes in. Now, you said you cut yourself on barbed wire. Are you up to date with your tetanus jabs?'

'I certainly am. The firm makes me have a medical every six months and they keep me up to date with things like that.'

'Good. Want another cup of tea?'

'Yes, please. But I think my blood-sugar levels are fine now. Could I have an unsweetened cup?'

'No problem. Then you just sit here for a while until Adam comes home. He shouldn't be more than three-quarters of an hour.'

Lyn fetched Ros's second cup and poured herself one. She was looking forward to having a chat with this woman. Ros was from a different world, a world that included Adam. Lyn wanted to know about it.

So far all she had noticed was that Ros was happy to spend money on herself. Not only was the car new, but Ros's clothes were as expensive as they had appeared. Her watch was a miracle of platinum technology, her rings, bracelet and earrings unobtrusive but suggesting considerable thought and expense.

'Have you known Adam long?' she asked Ros.

'All the time he's been working in TV. I've always been his producer. Of course, I work with other people but Adam is the one I like best. And the one who causes me most trouble.'

'Trouble? He seems very...pleasant to me.'

Ros laughed. 'Adam causes trouble in his own way. Everyone else I know, I work with, is anxious to get more exposure. They want to front this programme, got an idea for another one. But Adam isn't much bothered about appearing. I've got great plans for a new series, but is he interested? I'm working up here with a crew at the moment and I've grabbed the chance to come and pin him down, to talk to him. Have you seen his programmes, Lyn? He's good.'

'I've seen one or two. They're interesting.'

'He's a natural, he has great TV presence. He could be big but he'd rather be a doctor. And he's a wonderful man to work with. There's no side to him. In the bitchy world of TV, everybody likes him, and that's unusual.' Ros giggled. 'Not that he hasn't been known to take advantage of it.'

Lyn kept her head bowed. 'A bit of a ladies' man?' she asked in a muffled voice.

'Well, just a bit. You can't blame him. Wouldn't you do the same in those circumstances? But they all stay friendly with him after it's over.' Ros giggled again and Lyn realized she was still a little shocked. 'I've even had the odd moments of passion with him myself.'

'Very nice, too,' Lyn said levelly. 'Now, how are you feeling?'

'So much better. I must thank you and—'.

There was a knocking at the door. Lyn went to answer it and found Adam there. He smiled at her. 'Hi, Lyn. There's a car outside my house and I—'

She interrupted him, her voice cool. 'Your friend's

in here. She's hurt her hand. I've dressed it but you might like to take a look at it.'

Behind her she heard Ros approaching. 'Adam Fletcher! I've got you now, you're not escaping me. We're going to talk business whether you like it or not.'

She smiled at Lyn. 'Look, thank you so much for looking after me, I do appreciate it. But now I've got him I'm going to keep him. Adam! We're going to get things sorted.'

Adam looked resigned, his eyes swivelling between Lyn and Ros. 'Ros, you'd better come back to the house, I suppose. Lyn, I wanted to—'

'You've got work to do,' Lyn said crisply. 'Goodbye Ros, hope the hand is OK.' Then she shut the door.

She stood there a minute, hearing their voices from the other side.

Adam said, 'Look, Ros, it's good to see you but I really need to—'

And Ros said, 'You really need to talk to me. Now, let's go and get started.'

Then there was the rattle of footsteps fading away. Ros had got her way and Lyn was glad.

She went back into her living room and slumped into a chair. Adam was a womaniser. She should have guessed that a man as charming and good-looking as Adam could have his pick of women. It had been her own stupid fault, she should have known. But she still felt upset. She was disappointed, both with him and herself.

A couple of hours later there was another knock on her door. There were a smiling Ros and an anxious Adam.

'Ros is going to stay the night at the Red Lion,' Adam said. 'We're going there for a drink now. We'd both love it if you came, too.'

'I'd really like it if you came,' Ros said, 'so I could buy you a drink to say thank you.'

'I'm not in the mood for a drink,' Lyn said. 'Why doesn't Ros stay with you, Adam? I could even lend you some sheets. If they were needed.'

He looked as if he wanted to argue, but saw her set face. 'Ros will be happier at the Red Lion,' he said. 'Are you sure you don't want to—?'

'Yes, I'm sure,' she said. 'Goodnight, Ros.' Then she shut the door.

Feeling even more dissatisfied and angry, Lyn went back and turned on the TV. Nothing on there to interest her. She picked up a book, couldn't get into it. There was no music she wanted to listen to. This was turning into one of the worst evenings of her life.

Finally she went and had a bath. She poured half a jar of foaming something into it and then stayed there for much longer than normal, turning on the hot-water tap with her toe. How could she have been so stupid? At least she had found out in time what Adam was like. Otherwise she might have been just another woman in a long list of conquests. The very thought made her squirm. Why had she been tempted to come out of her shell? Why had she caused herself so much more misery?

Eventually she got out of her bath, put on a nightdress and dressing-gown and sat alone in the living room. No point in going to bed, she wouldn't sleep. She'd sit here and wait and perhaps eventually she might— Once again there was a knock at her door. At this hour of night?

It was Adam. They stood and surveyed each other in silence. He was unsmiling, but he looked determined.

'Yes?' she asked. The monosyllable hung in the air between them.

'May I come in? I won't be very long.'

She paused just long enough for him to know that she didn't really want him there, then silently led the way to her living room. She remained standing, so he had to do the same.

He looked round the room, as if trying to collect his thoughts. Then he said, 'I believe in frank talk. Most things can be explained by complete honesty, and I'd expect it from you. So tell me what's wrong.'

'Why should anything be wrong? Your friend's called, you've been for a drink and I—'

'Lyn! I deserve better than this. Just tell me what's wrong and then I'll go.' His voice was angry.

But she was angry, too. 'You deserve nothing from me. But I will tell you. Recently I've been getting quite…fond of you. I thought that you might be something new in my life. But one thing I will not be, and that's the latest in a long line of women.'

She hadn't realised just how angry she was. For most of the last three years she had taught herself to avoid emotion of any kind, to try to live a life detached from feelings. But now she was feeling. And it hurt.

'I suppose you think that because I'm a widow I'm easy game,' she snarled at him.

Then she stopped. She hadn't really meant to say that. But in her rage it had slipped out.

Adam's face whitened as if she had slapped him, and he half turned, as if to go. For a minute she felt ashamed, she hadn't intended to cause him so much pain. But what about the pain he had caused her?

Hoarsely he said, 'I never thought of you as any kind of game. I was always deadly serious. And never did I think that you were easy.'

He rocked backwards and forwards for a minute, his face closed as if he was thinking. She said nothing. There was nothing more to say.

Eventually he said, 'Let me guess. Ros told you I was a womaniser?'

'She hinted,' said Lyn. 'I gather she even had a brief fling with you herself.'

'Hmm. That cut on the hand must have affected her more than either she or I realised,' he said. 'She was more shocked than she knew. Usually she's the soul of discretion. She knows I'd sack her if I thought she was talking carelessly about me.'

For a minute she saw another, tougher Adam, whose existence she had only guessed at before.

He sighed. 'But I guess it's not her fault. Lyn, do you think we could sit down?'

She seated herself, silently indicating for him to do the same.

'I'm not a womaniser,' he said. 'Including Ros, I've had four relationships that you might call serious. That's in six years of working in television as an advisor and then a presenter. None of the women were what I hoped and expected to find—someone I could spend the rest of my life with.'

'Ros said that you've remained friends with them all.'

He looked puzzled. 'Well, yes. I'd like to think any of them could call on me for help. Just because something doesn't work out is no reason to drop someone.'

'I still think that four women in four years is rather a lot,' she said primly. 'I've had one lover in thirty-two years.'

'That's not fair! I could have had—'

Her mobile phone rang. There was no way she could ignore it.

The female voice was upset, even hysterical. 'Lyn, you've got to help me! This is Hetty Summers. I think the baby's coming and I'm alone at the farm.'

'I'll send for an ambulance, Hetty. Just take it easy and—'

'I can't leave the farm! Jack and Cathy are out. They've gone to the pictures and I'm supposed to be babysitting. I thought it was just another cramp at first but now I'm sure the baby's coming and—'

'I'll come round,' said Lyn. 'I'll be there in ten minutes. Just try to rest.' She rang off, looked up at Adam. 'Whatever we had to say to each other will have to wait.'

'What's the problem? You're the midwife but don't forget I'm a doctor.'

Lyn ran upstairs, peeled off her nightclothes and scrabbled for her uniform. 'Hetty Summers, living with her sister and brother-in-law at Longline farm,' she called down. 'She's eighteen years old, first baby, not married, father doesn't want to know. Poor Hetty's feeling a bit desperate. She's only thirty-seven weeks gone—I thought we'd have another three weeks but she thinks the baby is coming now. She can't send for an ambulance, she's babysitting for her sister's two young kids. I could turn out an ambulance and Social Services, but it'll save a lot of work if I go and check up on things.'

'I'll come with you.'

Now she ran downstairs, aware that she looked rather ruffled for a cool, competent midwife. 'No need. I'm a midwife, I've probably seen ten times the births you have.'

'I'd still like to come,' he said humbly. 'Perhaps I could boil the water or something. Anyway, I like babies.'

'Come on, then,' she said, now exasperated, 'though I don't know why you want to.'

'I'll just go next door and pick up my bag. I feel undressed without it. And I promise not to interfere unless I'm asked.'

'You'd better not.'

Longline Farm was high on the fells. First Lyn had to tackle a maze of back roads, then they bumped up the stony path, parked in the dark yard, passed by smells of cattle and made their way to the light shining from the open farmhouse door. As soon as they reached it they could hear the sound of groaning.

Hetty was lying on the couch, clutching her distended abdomen. 'Lyn, it's coming, I know it's coming,' she cried. 'The waters have broken and everything.'

'Where are the children, Hetty?' Adam asked.

'Top of the stairs, bedroom on the right. They were OK when I last— Ooh!'

'I'll just go and check,' Adam whispered to Lyn. 'Shout if I can help.'

She was pleased by the way he deferred to her expertise. This was her job.

Lyn got Hetty to lie out on the couch, placed a hand on her abdomen and winced. First, the waters had certainly broken. Second, the contractions were only about four minutes apart. Hetty's baby was coming fast.

'Why didn't you ring me sooner, Hetty?' she asked. 'You must have been in pain for quite some time.'

'Had some fried fish for my tea. I thought it was that that brought the pain on. Fried stuff doesn't agree with me, but I love it.'

Fortunately Hetty's bedroom was on the ground floor. Lyn half lifted the girl and supported her to her own bed. Hetty had dutifully followed Lyn's earlier advice, and all that was necessary for the new baby was stacked neatly to one side. Then Lyn walked out to speak to Adam. 'We're going to have a home delivery—and soon. I daren't send for an ambulance—all that bouncing about would mean the baby would be born before they got to hospital. Fetch all the stuff out of the boot of my car, will you? We're going to need it.'

As a matter of course Lyn carried all she might possibly need in the back of her car. Emergencies like this weren't too uncommon.

She stripped the bed, put on the coverings and undressed Hetty. Adam brought in her boxes and cases, opened the sealed packs and passed Lyn what she needed. He was a good nurse, anticipating her actions. Then he left as Lyn gave Hetty gas and air, showing her how to use the mask.

It might be an emergency—or a near emergency—but things had to be done according to protocol. Baseline observations first. Automatically Lyn took temperature, blood pressure, pulse and respiration rates. All were well within acceptable levels. Carefully she noted down her findings.

Next she listened to the baby's heart, holding the

Pinard's stethoscope firmly to her ear. A good healthy beat. Then an internal examination—head was at plus two.

Lyn slipped into the living room to find Adam. 'This is going to be one of those lightning babies, but all seems well. I'll need you to take the baby in a while, but until then there's no problem.'

'I'm here when you want me.'

As they talked they both heard a wail from upstairs. 'I'll go to see what I can do,' Adam said. 'With any luck I should be able to get whoever it is off to sleep again. Don't worry about anything.'

Lyn realised that he might have his uses after all.

The birth wouldn't be long. Lyn bathed Hetty's face, and in the moments of respite made sure that cot, basin and so on were ready. Adam drifted in and said, 'All quiet on the bedroom front upstairs. One small child accompanied to the toilet and now back in bed. How's Hetty?'

Now everything was under control Hetty was proving to be a perfect mother-to-be. It was to be a textbook birth, nothing was going wrong. At the right time Lyn called Adam, who pulled on a smock and stood ready to receive the child. Then he wrapped it—no, it was a him now—in the cloth Lyn held ready and placed the baby on Hetty's breast. 'He's a lovely baby, Hetty,' he said, and Lyn thought that she could hear real warmth in his voice.

There would be a certain amount of clearing up to do, but for the moment all was well. Lyn sat at a side table and filled in the Apgar form. Hetty's baby might have come somewhat quickly but he was a strong and healthy child.

'What are you going to call your baby, Hetty?' Lyn asked.

Hetty looked up from her child and for a moment her smile was replaced by a scowl. 'I'm going to call him Jamie,' she said defiantly. 'Jamie after Jamie Lennox, his dad. He might not want anything to do with me or his son, but he's going to give him his name.'

'He's a lovely baby,' Lyn said. She'd heard this kind of comment too often before to start to ask questions.

To Lyn's surprise Adam helped her with the cleaning and clearing up. Childbirth was a messy business and it was usually the midwife who cleaned away. But Adam was happy to help her. And just when they had finished they heard the rumble of a diesel engine outside.

Seconds later Hetty's sister and brother-in-law burst into the room.

'What's to do?' asked Jack.

'Not while we were out?' gasped his wife.

'It was easy,' said Hetty. 'Once I got started, that is.'

Lyn knew that Hetty was in good hands. Jack and Cathy were fond of Hetty, and would look after her and her child. Not every mother she saw was so lucky.

She decided that there was no need to stay the night. 'You've got my number,' she told Hetty, Jack and Cathy. 'Any problem whatsoever, ring me and I'll be here inside a quarter of an hour. Otherwise, I'll call first thing in the morning. But I don't think this little one is going to be any trouble.'

'Thanks a lot, Lyn,' Hetty called. 'And thank you, Doctor, too.'

'Jamie's a wonderful little lad, Hetty,' Adam said. 'I envy you.'

Lyn led him out to her car. 'You meant that about envying her, didn't you?' she asked as they swayed down the track. 'You were really taken with the baby.'

'He was a good strong boy, the sort of child any parent would be pleased with. I'd like to have one like that myself. In time, of course.'

'One?' she asked.

'Just to start with. I'd like at least one of each. But two's a small number, isn't it?'

'You can tell you're a man, and they don't have babies,' she told him. 'If you were a woman you might feel differently.'

'True. But isn't Hetty happy now?'

Adam was an odd man, Lyn thought as she eased the car out onto the main road. Most of her dads-to-be were happy about having a child—though some were a little apprehensive. But she had never met a man who was so committed to the idea of having children. That was usually a woman's thing. And Lyn felt certain that it wasn't just a wild idea on his part. When—and if—he had children, she knew he'd be a wonderful father.

'See, we're passing the Red Lion. Ros is in there asleep, not knowing what she's missed.' He paused a minute and said cautiously, 'Weren't we arguing when that call came?'

Lyn sighed. 'So we were. But it all seems unimportant now. Birth and so on puts it all in perspective.'

'So I'm forgiven?'

'There's nothing to forgive. My reaction was a bit

excessive, I know that now. It's just that I don't know where I am with you. I'm sorry.'

Adam leaned over and for a moment covered her hand on the steering-wheel with his. 'Lyn, I won't say that the women I knew were unimportant. At the time they were very important to me. I was always faithful and when we broke up I was sorry. But in every case we both realized that what...what I was looking for wasn't there. You might not believe it, but I envy that long relationship you had with Michael.'

'It was so good,' she said simply.

'I want something as good as that myself. And...I'm wondering if I'll find it with you.'

There was nothing she could say to that.

Afterwards Lyn wondered why it had happened that night. True, she'd had a hard day. There had been the misery and uncertainty when she'd thought Adam was a womaniser. Then there had been the sheer hard work of delivering Hetty's baby, and she had done a full day before that. She should have been exhausted, but for some reason she wasn't.

He pulled up outside her cottage and walked round to open the car door for her. She took the keys from him, turned irresolutely to her cottage door and then back to him.

'I suppose we're friends again now,' she said. 'You might as well come in and have a cocoa or something.' Then she thought over what she had just said, and giggled. 'Not the most enticing invitation, was it? Sorry. Please, let me make you a drink, Adam.'

'I'd really like that,' he said. 'I'd half forgotten what delivering babies was like.'

Lyn led him into her living room and switched on

a table lamp so the room was filled with a soft glow. Hetty's bedroom had been very brightly lit—fortunately—but now Lyn wanted something a little less glaring.

He agreed he would like cocoa, and she went to the kitchen to make it and to shake out the last few of her chocolate biscuits onto a plate. 'Pick out a CD,' she called, 'but something not too rousing. A bit of mood music.'

'Are you in the mood for love?' he called back, but she didn't reply. Moments later she heard a clear beautiful voice start one of her favourite romantic songs.

'And why did you pick that?' she asked as she came on with the drinks and biscuits. 'Not a hint, I trust?'

'I don't think there's a better song about the joys and possible miseries of love.'

'You're just an old romantic.' She smiled, 'Not really a hard-bitten doctor.'

'Doctors can be romantic, too. Well, I hope they can.'

He was sitting on her couch and it seemed natural to sit beside him. And for a while they drank, ate the biscuits and listened to the music.

The tension brought on by a very hard day slowly seeped away. But then there came another kind of awareness. She was sitting next to a very attractive man. His knee and thigh were close to hers, she could feel his warmth. She could see the movement of his chest as he breathed, smell the aftershave he used. They were alone together.

They both finished their drinks at once and leaned forward together to put their cups on the coffee-table. They smiled at the tiny coincidence. Then she saw his smile fade, to be replaced by a look whose meaning was unmistakable. She knew she could lean back or stand up or make some loud comment and all would be well. But instead, of their own volition, her eyes closed.

He kissed her. He put his arms round her body, pulled her to him and kissed her lips. At first he was gentle. But then, when she didn't resist—indeed, when she clutched him and pulled him even closer—his kiss grew much more demanding, and so much more exciting.

They sat there holding each other for—how long? She had no idea. But then he eased her away, only holding her two hands in his. His voice was hoarse, his breathing ragged. 'Perhaps I should go?' he said.

Some part of her could appreciate what he was doing, giving her this last chance to back away with her dignity intact. Did she want the chance? She considered.

Years of repression fought with every instinct that she had. She was Lyn Pierce, widowed midwife, she wanted nothing to do with men, she was fulfilled with her work. But she was also a woman. Both body and mind were telling her that this man was right for her. She wanted him, she needed him.

'Do you want to go?' She knew it was a foolish question as she asked it.

'No! I want to stay here with you. But I don't...I don't want to do or say anything that will spoil what we have between us. I desperately want to stay but only if you...'

She pulled him back to her, kissed him almost desperately. 'I'm frightened,' she confessed. 'But I know this is right for me and I know that it will get more right. Now...now...I want to go to bed.'

Had she said that? Part of her mind reeled at the sheer unlikelihood, the sheer horror of it.

She stood, still holding his hands, led him upstairs. This was her bedroom and for the past three years only she had entered it. There was a lamp on her dressing-table, and she clicked it on to show the white sheets on the double bed, the bedside bookcase, the little radio she listened to when she could treat herself to an extra half-hour in bed. This was her own little world and she was inviting Adam into it.

She was still wearing her uniform. He reached for her tunic, lifted it over her head. Then he reached behind her, unfastened her bra. She stood before him, thrilling to his sigh of excitement, the glint in his eyes. His hands cupped her face, then his fingers traced a double line down her neck, the line of her shoulders, the sensitive spot on the insides of her arms.

She could feel her breathing getting faster, could feel her heart beating. When, very delicately, he touched her breasts, she felt them tighten, the peaks erect against the warmth of his palms.

He crossed his arms, swiftly pulled off his shirt. Then he took her to him, crushing her breasts to the muscles of his chest, kissing her with a passion that excited her.

Now Lyn knew the full force of his urgency. His hands hooked into her trousers, pushed them down, together with her panties, so that she was naked before him. He bent, slipped an arm under her knees and lifted her onto the bed, ignoring her little squeak of alarm. And he, too, was naked, poised above her.

But then he twisted to lie beside her and kissed her again. And his lips roamed downwards, taking, caressing her breasts, then moving even lower so her back arched and she had to stop herself from screaming in ecstasy.

But this wasn't fair! She grabbed for Adam's arm, pulled him so once again he was on top of her.

'Lyn darling—I haven't got any...'

She nodded and indicated her medical bag by the bed. 'Free samples in there.'

As he retrieved a foil packet, Lyn reflected on the bitter irony of the situation, but she pushed it out of her mind. She still had hope.

'Make love to me,' she whispered.

Was this Lyn Pierce talking?

For a while longer he was there. Then he lowered himself onto her, into her, and she gasped with delight.

They fitted so well together. They weren't two bodies but one and each knew, felt what the other needed. And they were so excited, it couldn't take long. And she knew as she screamed with climactic excitement that he was there with her.

'Sweetheart,' he whispered as he lay by her. 'That's never happened to me before.'

'Nor me. But go to sleep now,' she mumbled. 'We can talk in the morning.'

It was good to wake with the warmth of a man's body beside her. It was comforting, reassuring. She always woke early, when the first fingers of sunlight were creeping into her room, but, instead of thinking about the day ahead, this time she was content just to lie there. Adam was next to her and that was all she needed.

Then a voice beside her said, 'I can feel you looking at me. Are you all right?'

'I'm fine. I feel happy.' Lyn rolled onto her side, put an arm round him and hugged his back. 'I was just thinking, these cottages must be haunted. What happened to us happened to Jane and Cal, too. Well, she sort of told me.'

'It must be the nicest ghost I've ever come across. We'll find out who lived here. I'll bet it was a happily married woman blessed with fifteen kids. Encouraging other women to have the same.'

'With fifteen kids she wouldn't be haunting. She'd be having a rest. And fifteen kids isn't a blessing, it's a curse.'

'Well, certainly hard work,' he said thoughtfully. 'Five is a nice number, isn't it?'

'I'm too sleepy for this kind of conversation, I think I'll go back to sleep for a while. D'you want a cup of tea or anything?'

He rolled onto his back. 'I don't want any tea. But if you like, we could…'

She removed an exploring hand. 'Adam!' Then she giggled. 'I was just going to say that I hardly know you. But, then…'

'We do hardly know each other. But I'm really looking forward to getting to know you. Starting right now.'

His hand was wandering again so, although she liked it, she slipped out of bed and pulled on her dressing-gown. 'I'll fetch you some tea, and then you'd better go home before the neighbours are up.'

She fetched the tea, although it was largely an excuse to get out of bed. She knew what would happen if she stayed there. When she returned she sat on the bed and said, 'We're neighbours ourselves. We'll be seeing a lot of each other. But I'm still a bit unsure about things.'

He nodded. 'I know that.' His voice was serious now. 'We need to get things straight. First, we both know that what happened last night wasn't just sex, don't we?'

She blushed. 'Well, I certainly know. You took me to places I'd never been before. And I want to go there again. But we have time to get to know each other.'

'That's fine.' He put down his cup and stretched an arm round her naked shoulders. 'We've got time, but I don't think it'll take too long.'

She'd finished her drink. It was still very early, perhaps she'd just snuggle down and wait a few minutes before getting up. And now he had one arm round her neck and the other round her waist, was easing her under the sheet again, was reaching across her.

'Adam, you really ought to go home. It'll soon be time to...'

Perhaps they did have enough time.

CHAPTER SIX

FINALLY, after more ecstatic love-making, Adam did go. And it was still very early. Unbelievably—or perhaps not—Lyn managed to sleep for a while when he had gone. Well, she'd had an eventful past few hours.

But then she was still up early, and happy, and wandered downstairs as if the world was somewhere new and she wanted to make the most of it while she could.

After a quick breakfast she drove over to see Hetty and her new little boy. As Hetty lived on a farm, Lyn knew that there'd be someone up. It was another wonderful morning, with the trees getting the early brown tinge of autumn.

As she drove she remembered when she had visited Julie and Bill on their farm, on her way to take the papers to Adam. That, too, had been a glorious day, but her mood had been different. She had felt melancholy, her life had seemed boring and even. She hadn't met Adam then.

It seemed odd to think of a time when she hadn't known him. He had made such a difference to her life! It wasn't boring and even any more, it was…different. It was going to change. But right now she didn't want to think, to plan. She just wanted to be, to feel. Life was good.

She found a smiling Jack in the farmyard, who said mother and child had spent a quiet night. Lyn went inside, found a smiling Hetty and Cathy, and the squalling infant. There were the normal observations to be written up, arrangements to be made. But so far little Jamie seemed to have a good start in life. Lyn left, promising to drop in again that evening.

She was back in surgery again in time for the casual morning meeting. Adam was already there. She wondered if the others noticed the slight colour that tinged her cheeks when she saw him.

'I've just been telling people about our exciting night,' Adam said smoothly. 'About being with you when Hetty Summers phoned. I enjoyed working with you. How's Hetty this morning?'

'Mother and child doing fine,' Lyn said, trying to keep her voice steady. 'Hetty sent word to thank you for what you did.'

She was aware of the interested glances from the other members of staff. As an experienced midwife, for an uncomplicated birth she shouldn't have needed a doctor in attendance. But, then, Adam was new to the practice. Perhaps they thought he'd just been getting experience.

At that moment Adam's mobile rang. When he started work he would hand it over to the receptionist, but now he could answer it.

'Oh, Hi, Ros,' Lyn heard him say. 'Sleep well? Yes, fine. I know we've got things to sort out but I'm a doctor now... Look, as soon as I've finished my day I'll come round to the Red Lion and we can spend all evening talking... Yes, that's fine.'

He turned, raised his eyebrows at Lyn. She got the message. Adam couldn't see her tonight. Well, there would be other nights. But she was rather disappointed.

She had a clinic all that morning, and then went

home before setting out on her afternoon calls. She often did this when she had time to spare. She could do a bit of tidying. Perhaps she could do some thinking, too.

There was a pile of mail inside her door. Much of it was advertising material from medical firms and went straight in the bin. But there was a thick letter from the Leeds hospital, and when she saw it Lyn tensed. She had put from her mind the question she had asked Mr Smilie. But now that question was more important to her than ever.

She didn't open it at once. Instead, she placed it in the middle of her coffee-table. There were other things she had to do, and she would do them first. There were notes to be written up, appointments to be checked, the bits of tidying she had promised herself. But finally she could find no more excuses. She made herself a drink and placed that on the table, too. Then she sat down and opened the letter.

She was a fellow professional and, knowing she would want to understand, Mr Smilie had sent the detailed results of all the tests. And there was a personal letter from him. She could take other tests, perhaps seek a second opinion. He was very sorry to have to tell her this, but he doubted whether she would ever be able to conceive. Mechanically Lyn read and reread the letter. This just couldn't be happening to her! Suddenly it was all so important!

She found herself looking at the picture of her dead husband, hoping for inspiration. When he'd first died she'd talked to that picture—it had been like talking to Michael himself. It had helped, she had heard the remembered voice speak back. But now she realised there would be no reply. Finally he had left her, she was now on her own. The picture was just part of her memories.

She was calm, and this surprised her. Then she realised the calmness was to hide her panic. She had to think.

Adam was now part of her life. They both had agreed—last night had been much more than sexual. It had been a beginning of something, a promise of more. All right, they had decided to take their time, not to hurry things, and quite possibly they might find that they were not right for each other. But she knew this was rubbish. Adam and she were made for each other. And so in time—probably not too much time—inevitably they would think of marriage. And that for him meant children.

Everything she knew about him, everything he had ever said told her that he wanted, he needed children. And she couldn't have them.

She knew she couldn't tell him about the letter. Now she knew him well, she could predict his reply. He would say that it didn't matter, that he loved her, that he wasn't bothered that she couldn't have children. He might even believe it. But she couldn't allow him to make that sacrifice. In time he would feel differently.

It was a bitter irony. She had thought that she would never feel this way again, That there was no chance that she would ever fall in love again. But she had. And now she had to lie to the man she loved. Well, he would be gone in a few months. There would be nothing for him here.

As she thought this she heard a car draw up outside. She peered through the window—and there was Adam, getting out of his car. Looking at him, she thought her heart would burst. Why did he have to come now? She grabbed the letter from the coffee-table, quickly ran into the kitchen and hid it in a cupboard. She didn't want the letter in the same room as them.

Adam knocked, and when Lyn let him in he seized her and kissed her. Holding him felt so good that for a moment she was tempted to forget the letter, just to let things fall out how they might. But she couldn't do that. Not to a man she loved.

'I've got half an hour,' he said, 'and I just wanted to see you alone. This evening I have really to spend with Ros, so I wanted to see you while I could.'

'Do you want a coffee?' she asked coolly.

'No. I just want to sit, to be with you.'

He led her unresisting to the couch, but once there she managed to ease herself away from his arms, to sit at one end while he was at the other. 'Adam! We've got to talk. If you're doing that you'll distract me.'

'I like distracting you.'

'Well, we're moving too fast. We need to stop, to take stock.'

'Stocktake away. I'm all yours. All yours, Lyn.'

That wasn't what she wanted to hear. And when she looked at his face she didn't know how she would be able to carry on.

'I've been thinking. First of all, last night was fantastic. I have no regrets. You are a wonderful lover and you made me so happy, happier than I've been in years.'

She saw he was about to speak, so hurriedly she went on, 'Please, let me finish. I don't love you. I don't want to love you, I've been in love and it hurts too much. I'm not going through that again. You'll be leaving here in a few months, I'm never going to move. So we'll have to part then. And until then we see each other, we keep on being friends, perhaps we even sleep together again. This is just a casual affair. And when we part, we part with no regrets, no recriminations.'

When Lyn had started to speak she had seen that he was upset. But then his face became thoughtful, and this worried her. She wanted him to accept, not to think.

'What happened?' he asked. 'Why are you different from this morning?'

This was too shrewd! 'Nothing's happened,' she said quickly. 'I've just had the chance to think a bit.'

'But two nights ago you were angry with me because you thought I was a womaniser. Now you want me to be one—and with you! That's not like you.'

She shrugged, hoping to convince him. 'It's the way it is, Adam. This morning was this morning. Now is now. Just one thing. Never say you love me. I've been in love, I don't want it again. If you ever say you love me, then everything between us is over. Can we get that straight now?'

He looked at her, and it was the hardest thing she had ever done to keep her face serene. But somehow she did. She didn't know what he was thinking. For once his usually transparent face was enigmatic.

'As you wish,' he said. 'And now I suppose I'd better go. I've calls to make.'

She waited till she heard his car drive away. Then she went upstairs, fell forward onto the bed where they had so recently made love. Her face was pressed against the pillow where his head had rested and there was the faintest aroma of his expensive aftershave, of his body even. She wept, more bitterly than she had done since her husband had died.

'This is for you,' Hetty said, 'for you and Dr Fletcher. I made it myself, I wanted to give you a good one.'

It was three days later. Lyn was again at Longline Farm, checking up on Hetty's and young Jamie's progress. They were both doing fine and Cathy looked on approvingly.

Lyn unwrapped a corner of the flat parcel and peered into it. It was a cheese, made by hand at the farm.

'We sell them at the farmers' market,' Hetty's sister said. 'They do very well. And we sell a lot to the local hotels as well.'

Lyn was often offered gifts like this. Sometimes it was something simple, like a box of chocolates or a bottle of wine. But occasionally it was something home-grown or home-made, which she enjoyed even more.

'It smells wonderful,' Lyn said honestly, 'I'll give half to Dr Fletcher and have some for my tea.'

'Doesn't Dr Fletcher ever have his tea with you?' Hetty asked interestedly. 'He lives next door to you, doesn't he?'

'Well, yes, but—'

Someone knocked on the door, much to Lyn's relief. The door opened and a rather shamefaced youth looked round it. 'All right to come in?'

'Come in, Jamie,' Cathy said cheerfully. 'Lyn here's the midwife. She's just checking up on the baby for a couple of minutes and then we'll leave you three alone for a while.'

Jamie came in, nearly tripped over a chair as he passed, then looked down at the baby at Hetty's breast. Gingerly, he leaned forward to stroke the back of the little head.

'Jamie here is little Jamie's father,' Hetty said flatly.

Lyn didn't smile, simply looked up. In her profession she had met—or often not met—too many fathers who wouldn't face up to their responsibilities. She didn't like them. 'Come to see your son Jamie?' she asked him.

'Yes. Think he's…he's lovely. It took a bit of getting used to the idea, but we're…we're…'

'Me and Jamie are getting together for good,' Hetty said. 'We're hoping to move into a little flat, perhaps get a council house in time. But getting anywhere to live round here is hard.'

'I'm very pleased to hear you're getting together,' said Lyn. 'A baby needs a mother and a father. And I know about property prices.' But then she remembered the many hours of tears from Hetty when Jamie had been nowhere to be seen. 'Why the sudden change of heart, Jamie?'

'When she heard, my mum made me come to see the baby. And when I saw him, and when Hetty said he was going to be called Jamie, then I had to, didn't I? He's a little me.'

Lyn thought he seemed genuinely moved. And, like Hetty, he was so young! Feeling a thousand years old, she said, 'Babies aren't always like this, you know. They wake up at night, they get sick, they need lots of looking after. Babies can be hard work.'

'I know that. But I've sat up that many times with

my dogs that I think I can sit up with a baby, too. And my sister's had three, I know what they're like.'

'Well, I'll leave you to it, then. Bye, Hetty, I'll be in again next week.'

Lyn took her cheese and walked across the yard. Jack was there and walked over to have a quick word.

'I gather young Jamie's father has had a change of heart,' she said.

Jack nodded. 'I think he'll be a good father. I know about him. He's wonderful with animals, really patient. If he wanted to work for me I'd find somewhere for them both to live. Then everyone would profit.'

'Sounds a good idea.' Lyn smiled. 'Hope it all works out well.'

As she drove off down the bumpy road she wondered why her problems weren't so easy to solve.

That evening she cut the cheese and carried half round to Adam. He was just leaving, carrying a thick file, and he said he had another dinner date with Ros. 'I'd love you to come,' he said, 'but we'll be doing nothing but work. Ros can be a slave-driver, and she claims she's behind schedule.'

'That's fine. I like workers, and I've got some form-filling to do myself. I've just brought you this cheese. Perhaps you'd like to take a bit for Ros? And I've got a story with a happy ending.' She told him about Jamie and Hetty.

He was thoughtful. 'D'you think they'll stick together?'

She considered. 'Probably yes. I suspect they will make a go of it, though it might be hard.'

'People can sort out their problems,' he said. 'All they need is a bit of honesty and confidence. Now, I must go.'

She watched him walking down the lane, and wished she could walk with him.

For a further three days she hardly saw him. In some ways it was relief, in others it was a torture. When they met in the surgery they had to remain distant but friendly—and she didn't know if she was getting it right. Then one evening there was a knock on her door and she opened it to find Ros and Adam.

'I'm taking Adam down to dinner at the Red Lion and putting it on expenses,' Ros said. 'Will you come as well? I haven't thanked you properly for dressing my hand when I cut it.'

So she went with them. It was good to be with Adam and, because Ros was there as well, she wouldn't be tempted to feel things that were forbidden.

They chatted about work on television, a closed world to Lyn. 'You would look great on the screen,' Ros said. 'You've got a good TV face. It's heart-shaped, it would show up, be attractive. The camera puts weight on people, but you're slim enough to get away with that. I'm sorry we can't film you.'

'It's just not me anyway,' Lyn said.

They were waiting for their meal to be served, and Ros went outside to use her mobile. 'That was interesting,' Lyn said to Adam. 'Ros was very flattering about me, but she was quite detached. I felt that if I'd been too fat she would have said so in exactly the same voice.'

'Probably,' he agreed. 'Ros is a very nice person, but she's a consummate professional. Were you interested in what she had to say?'

'Very much so. I've seen a new side of you, too.

You're a professional on TV, as Ros is. You're good at it and you enjoy it. In a few months you know you'll be back to it.'

He shook his head. 'I'm thinking that my future might be around here, Lyn. I'm getting more and more involved with this outreach clinic scheme of Cal's. I'd like to help develop it, see it through. Perhaps in time even open another one. And there's another reason why I want to stay. You know that.'

'I've got another round of drinks in,' said Ros as she rejoined them.

CHAPTER SEVEN

'You said you had a new mast for your boat,' Adam said the next day. 'And you promised to take me sailing one day. How about Saturday? I've checked the rosters and neither of us are on call over the weekend. If the weather's good, I'd love a sail.'

Lyn thought about it. Being with him would be so painful—it would remind her of what she could not have. On the other hand, being without him would just make her miserable.

'Just a couple of friends going for a sail together?' she asked.

'What else? You've told me what fun it is. If you're right, I'll think of getting a boat myself.'

'OK, then, I'll take you. We can borrow a lifejacket from the club.'

'We could meet there if you like. I've got some work to do on my laptop, so I've hired a cruiser just for the weekend. It's peaceful out on the lake, it's easy to work there.'

'Aren't you peaceful next door?'

'Too peaceful. I want to be disturbed but I'm not.'

Lyn didn't answer that but she knew exactly what he'd meant. It would be no consolation to him to know that she felt exactly the same way.

As she drove over on Saturday morning she thought of how her life had changed since she had driven to the lake and met Adam for the first time. How *had* it changed? And was it for the better? She was now much more unsettled and knew that never again would she be as she'd been before.

She realised her life before she'd met Adam had been in a shadow. Now her life was in the sunlight again. The trouble was, though, that now she had the ability to enjoy herself more, she could also suffer more. Meeting Adam had brought both happiness and pain. And at the moment pain was in the ascendant. Still, she was spending the day with him. She would enjoy that.

He was waiting for her at the club, dressed in shorts and an old shirt. She changed in the clubhouse, borrowed him a lifejacket and showed him how to rig the dinghy.

'She's called the *Start Again*,' Adam said curiously. 'That's an unusual name. Why not the *Pretty Polly* or *Saucy Sue*?'

'Silly! She isn't pretty or saucy.' She tightened one of the halliards then said, 'I bought her just after my husband died. I had to do something new or I thought I'd go mad. And I called her *Start Again* because that was what I had to do.'

'I see. I'm sorry if my question caused you pain.'

She smiled. 'It didn't. And I have started my life again. I'm happy now.' She considered. 'Well, happier. Now, let's get this thing launched.'

He put his hand over hers. 'You've got a new mast as the old one broke. Perhaps you should change the name and change the boat's luck. Call it *Start Again Two*. When your mast snapped you were coming to see me. My life changed then. I'd like to think that yours did, too.'

'My life did change,' Lyn said after a pause. 'But

how it changed I'm still not sure. But I'll stick a "two" after the *Start Again.*'

There was a reasonable wind and they pushed off. Lyn told Adam where to sit, how to sit out, how to hold the jib sheets. At first they only drifted as they were in a wind shadow, but when they reached the bay, the wind blew, the boat heeled and he looked comically worried.

'Is this safe?' Adam called.

'Oh, it's safe all right. But is it fun?'

'It's more than fun, it's marvellous. Just how fast are we going?'

She grinned. Lots of people were surprised at the illusion of speed. 'Not more than seven knots,' she called back. 'You could run faster. Now, concentrate on what we do when I turn into the wind.'

They had a good run across the lake, then Lyn headed for a quieter spot, made Adam take the helm and gave him a lesson. She was enjoying herself, it did her good to have to teach things. And he was a quick study. He had naturally sensitive hands, could respond to the wind and the feel of the tiller. She knew those hands. So sensitive, so gentle and yet so certain…

'Now who's not concentrating?' came his cheerful shout.

They enjoyed themselves. She lost herself in just being with him, in the sun, on the water, doing something together that was fun. For a moment there was no need to worry about the future. She was together with a man whom she…very much liked.

Eventually, when it was late afternoon, they sailed back to the club and he helped her take down the mast and haul the dinghy onto its trailer.

'Do you have to go back?' he asked. 'I've got the cruiser tied up at the jetty. You could join me for a meal if you wished.'

He didn't push her, she noticed. It was a gentle, friendly invitation. So she accepted. Whatever the consequences, she would take them. 'I'd like a meal on board,' she said. 'And could we go for another cruise?'

She remembered there was a shower on board, so she showered and changed into the trousers, blouse and sweater she had been wearing earlier. Then they cast off, and the cruiser set out onto the lake. By now it was dusk. The distant peaks were just a dark edge against the red evening sky and lights were appearing on the banks, like decorations on a Christmas tree. It was beautiful.

After her day on the water she was tired, it was good to sit beside Adam in the cockpit and relax.

'No commitments at all tonight?' he asked softly. 'No time you have to be back by?'

Lyn hesitated before answering. This was a way out, an excuse. But she replied, 'I'm not needed at home till Monday morning.' She had said it now. The die was cast.

But all he said was, 'I've got supplies for as long as we need them. Whatever happens, we won't starve.'

So they made their slow way down the lake. She moved to sit next to him, and he steered with one hand, putting the other arm round her shoulders. They watched the passing shoreline, feeling there was no need to talk.

It became cool on the water. Lyn shivered and he

pulled off his coat and draped it round her shoulders. 'No need, I'll fetch my jacket,' she said.

'Stay where you are. I like you next to me.' So she stayed. She liked the feel, the smell of his coat. It was him.

Suddenly it grew much colder, and she felt the wind shake the boat. 'Every time we go out,' he said, 'there's a storm. D'you think Mother Nature is telling us something?'

'She's telling me to keep warm,' said Lyn. 'Thanks for the coat but I need my sweater now.'

'Perhaps it's time we had our meal. Now, there's a place near here where there's a mooring we can use. Want to grab that boat hook and pick it up? Look, it's that yellow float.'

So she picked up on the boat hook and, as Adam slowed the cruiser, deftly pulled it aboard. She had done this kind of thing before and it was the work of only a minute to fasten the cruiser to the mooring chain. Then she dropped back into the cockpit.

He had seen her obvious expertise and had shut down the engine and moved forward into the little galley to start work. She offered to set the table, and within ten minutes their meal was ready. She guessed he must have done most of the preparation before, probably at home. There was a rocket salad with Gorgonzola, hot bacon strips and tiny pieces of avocado, then saffron rice with a creamy chicken sauce. And finally two wonderfully sticky Rum babas.

'I cheated with the pudding,' he confessed with a grin. 'I've never been too good on sweet stuff, so I bought these early this morning.'

'I'll teach you how to bake cakes,' Lyn said, licking her fingers. 'Though these are wonderful.'

With the meal they had a bottle of chilled white wine, and when they had finished, they took their glasses out into the cockpit again. It was dark now, but by some unspoken agreement they decided not to turn on the cockpit light.

It had stopped raining, but the wind was high and the cruiser rocked. Lighting flashed and forked its way overhead. For a moment the lake, the wooded banks, the other moored boats were outlined in black and bleached white. Then there was complete darkness again, and the crack and rolling of thunder. And still it didn't rain.

'I think we're going to have a dry storm,' she said after a while. 'It happens sometimes. And it's a pity, because we need the rain.'

'We must enjoy what we are given,' Adam said. 'I'm enjoying this.'

She wondered if he was talking about the storm or something else, but decided not to question him.

He put his arm round her. She moved closer to him and his body warmed her. The lightning show continued and they saw it strike one of the peaks by the lake. Then slowly it passed, moving down the valley.

'That was so exciting,' she breathed. 'My heart's beating faster, I feel as if things are different now.'

'Things are different? I feel just the same. That is, I feel just the same about you.'

He put down his glass on the table, she heard its tiny ting. Then he reached for her, took her to him and kissed her. She knew this was what she wanted! Her arms went round him and she kissed him back, aware of his growing need for her.

She had slipped her hand under his shirt. Now she tugged at it, pulling it upwards. Her fingertips traced the twin columns of muscle down his spine, her thumb reached into the warmth under his arm. But she couldn't touch him with her other hand. With a little sigh of annoyance she released him, took his shirt in her two hands, pulled it over his head and threw it to one side.

She could see the whiteness of his body, but couldn't see his expression. She laid her hands flat on his chest, stroked him and felt his warmth, the silkiness of the hair on his chest. When her hands grazed his nipples she heard him sigh, felt him flinch.

'And you're supposed to be a big strong man,' she whispered playfully.

'I am a big strong man. But it seems that you can do anything to me. Now I want to see how you react when I touch you.'

Her shirt buttoned all the way down her front. He started at the top, and with maddening patience undid the buttons one by one. Then, still slowly, he took the blouse from her and threw it on top of his own.

With his two hands he cupped her face, kissed her. And, still kissing her, he in turn let his finger tips roam down her neck, caress her shoulders and trace the line along the top of her lacy bra.

'I'm a doctor,' he breathed after a while. 'There are things I shouldn't notice.'

'You're not a doctor now, you're a man. What shouldn't you notice?'

'When you fell into the water and I dragged you out and undressed you. I saw that you had a beautiful body. I also saw that you wore rather nice underwear.'

Lyn giggled. 'My one vice. Just ordinary clothes or my uniform for everyday. But I do like lacy things underneath.' She paused a moment and then said reproachfully, 'If you like my underwear, why are you taking off my bra?'

He said nothing, but dropped the garment on top of her blouse. Then he bent his head to her naked breasts and she thrilled at the touch of his tongue.

She couldn't tell how much longer they remained in each other's arms as the lightning slowly diminished and the thunder calmed to a distant mutter. Time had no meaning. They were both wrapped in the glorious present with no need to worry about the past or think about the future.

But then Adam spoke. 'Will you come with me, Lyn? Come to my cabin with me.'

'Of course I will, sweetheart. I want to.'

He took her hand and led her below. She remembered his cabin and thought she had never seen anything so appealing. There was his double bunk with the crisp white sheets, the brass portholes, the little shelf of books. The cabin was darker now, lit only by a bedside lamp that cast shadows and made things seem more mysterious.

For a while they stood by the bed, their arms round each other, content merely to press against each other. She felt calm and excited at the same time. She loved being here with him. And she wanted what she knew would happen next.

Soon they were both naked. They lay on the bed together, clung to each other with a passion that led quickly to a frantic, groaning climax. She felt she was out of time, giving herself to this man entirely, offering him all of herself. And by giving, she was able to take, too. Never had she had a climax like this!

But then it was over, and there was the equally wonderful drowsy calm. And time came back, she was in the real world again and responsible for her actions and aware of the future.

'Lyn, Lyn,' he muttered. 'You know I'm—'

She stopped his mouth with a kiss. 'You're getting very fond of me,' she said. 'And I'm very fond of you. No other words are needed. We're fond of each other.'

'But I feel it and I want to say it! I've never felt like this before and I—'

'I'm a very demure lady, Adam. And for me love is a four-letter word. We don't say it, we don't think it. If you talk to me about love, then I must go.'

She couldn't bear to see the pain and puzzlement in his eyes, so she pulled him close to her, hung her neck over his shoulder and squeezed her own eyes tight shut, so there would be no tell-tale tears.

It was so hard not to shout out the words that came unbidden to her lips. *I love you, too.* But she knew she had to keep silent.

Four nights later Lyn was in her cottage when Jane called in, Helen by her side. When they were sitting down Helen proudly gave her an envelope.

'It's an invitation to a party,' she said. 'But there are no balloons on the envelope. I had balloons on my party envelopes for my last birthday. I was three.'

Lyn opened the envelope and looked first with delight and then with dismay at the silver printed card inside. 'Miss Jane Hall and Dr Calvin Mitchell are celebrating their engagement to be married and request the company of...'

Jane had obviously been pleased at Lyn's initial squeak of delight but was now puzzled by her frown. 'Is there something wrong?' she asked. 'You can come, can't you? I must have you there. I want you to come so much.'

'Of course I can come, nothing would keep me away. But this invitation is to Adam and me. As a couple. We're not a couple, Jane, we're just good friends.'

She knew she reddened slightly as she told this lie.

Jane's reply was robust. 'Don't be silly, Lyn. I've seen the way he looks at you, and the way you look at him. You can't hide anything from Auntie Jane. He's besotted by you.'

Lyn coloured even more. 'I like him a lot, I really do. But nothing...will come of it. Nothing can come of it. He's just not my type and—'

'Lyn, you don't get a second chance at a man like Adam! There aren't many of them about. Grab him while you can, like I did with Cal.'

Lyn shook her head in distress. 'No, Jane, it just won't work. He's not for me. Take my word for it, I know.'

Jane looked at her friend closely. 'Whatever you say. I don't think you're telling me the whole story, but just so long as you know that if you want any advice, then I'm here for you. You know what I think—I think he's marvellous. Now, do I have to go and write out two more invitations?'

'No,' Lyn said gloomily, 'I'll sort it out myself.'

'It's going to be a big get-together type of party,' Jane said encouragingly. 'Once you're there you can talk to whoever you want. We're having a big marquee on the back lawn.'

'Should be great,' said Lyn.

She heard Adam come in about an hour after Jane and Helen had left, and went straight next door to show him the invitation. Somehow he divined what she was thinking. 'An invitation to both of us. Perhaps it's because we live next door to each other.'

'Or perhaps it's because they think we're a couple. Which we're not.'

'Whatever you say. Still, it sounds fantastic and I'm looking forward to it. I like the occasional big knees-up.'

He smiled at her, and his obvious enthusiasm only made her feel more depressed. 'What shall we get them for a present? Something for what used to be called the bottom drawer?'

'I don't think we should get a joint present,' she said flatly. 'I'll help you pick something if you like but I want us to give presents separately. If we give something together, it will make people think and talk.'

'Whatever you want.'

He kept his bantering smile but his eyes told her that he was hurt by her decision. But it had to be. A joint present for an engagement party might give him ideas, as well as other people.

The party was a week later. Lyn went to Cal's house early to keep an eye on Helen while Jane supervised. Helen, of course, was madly excited and was already calculating the years before she too could get engaged. 'I'll be sixteen in thirteen years,' she said. 'And Uncle Cal said you can get married at sixteen.'

'I'd wait a while if I were you,' Lyn advised. 'Would you have an engagement party exactly like this?'

Helen considered. 'I'd want more balloons,' she

said. 'And I'd want them in different colours. But otherwise just the same.'

It was going to be a wonderful party, not least because of the weather. It was still unseasonably warm and Lyn could hardly remember the last time it had rained.

Jane had wondered if it all could be organised in time, but Cal knew everybody locally and had found the best team for everything. It seemed no time before the marquee was erected, the flooring down inside and the tables and chairs arranged. Then the caterers came with their portable kitchen, which was soon producing the most wonderful smells. Then the band arrived.

Helen ran everywhere, checked everything, until finally Lyn managed to lure her indoors for a bath. 'We can put your new party dress on,' she said. 'You want to look smart for everyone.'

The party was to start at eight. Helen was bathed, dressed and sitting watching television when Lyn slipped into the bedroom she had borrowed and put on her own dress. Jane had pushed her into buying something new—indeed, had dragged her into Keldale and stood over her till she bought something.

'I'm not dressing up for anyone special,' she had protested to Jane. 'Apart from you and Cal, of course.'

'You always dress up for someone special' had been the sharp reply. 'You dress up for yourself. And at my engagement party I want you looking good.'

Perhaps it wasn't the dress Lyn would have bought herself, but as she surveyed herself in the full-length mirror, she had to say that she looked good.

It was dark red, in a very fine wool mix that clung

to her. It was sleeveless, almost backless. Lyn had muttered that it was nearly frontless, too. It was slashed from the hem to her right thigh.

'If you've got it, flaunt it,' Jane had advised. 'Only a woman with a figure like yours could get away with a dress like that.'

'There doesn't seem to be much dress for such a big price,' Lyn had said. But both in the boutique and here, she knew it was the dress for her.

Out of cowardice she took a white wrap with her, there might be circumstances when she'd feel more comfortable with it thrown round her shoulders. Then she went to collect Helen and take her to Jane and Cal. And ten minutes later she went to the party herself.

Her feelings were mixed. She was happy for Jane and Cal, very much looking forward to meeting so many old friends and indeed new ones. But she just didn't know how she would deal with Adam.

She had explained that she couldn't arrive at the party with him as she was needed to look after Helen.

'I'll see you there, then,' he had said, and she had left it at that.

The guests were arriving promptly as this party wasn't going to go on too late. She accepted a glass of champagne from a waiter and went forward to be formally greeted by Jane, Cal and a very formal Helen.

'You're already turning heads,' Jane whispered. 'That dress is really something.'

'Just the thing for the district midwife,' Lyn muttered back. 'I feel like the district scarlet woman.'

'A bit of scarlet behaviour wouldn't hurt you. Or are there things you haven't been telling me?'

As Lyn reddened yet again, it struck her that she had blushed more in the past few weeks than she had in the previous five years. What was happening to her?

'Could I interrupt this obviously ladies' conversation?' came Cal's amiable voice. 'There's someone I'd like Lyn to meet. Lyn, this is Josh Harrison. He's going to be one of our registrars and he'll be joining us in a few weeks. Josh, this is Lyn, our midwife. Take it from me, she's good.'

They used to be called trainees, now they were called registrars. Newly qualified doctors who wanted to be GPs had to spend three years with a practice, learning the practical side of things. Cal was a known and respected trainer, and there were always plenty of applicants wanting to work with him.

Lyn shook hands and thought she was going to like working with Josh. He was younger than her, of course, and he seemed very pleasant.

'Jane and I have to carry on welcoming people,' Cal went on. 'Josh only found out today that he could make it here, so d'you think you could show him round, introduce him to everyone?'

'Be pleased to,' Lyn said. She was rather taken by the way Josh's eyes had lit up when he'd seen her— or saw the dress. Normally she would have been pleased to show him round, but she'd rather have been with Adam. 'Where are you from, Josh?'

'Well, actually, I guess I'm a local.'

After that it was easy. He had gone to a neighbouring school, they had friends and acquaintances in common, and as she introduced him to other members of the practice she knew he was going to fit in.

And then, suddenly, there was Adam. She turned

and he was beside her, looking amazing in his dinner jacket. His smile was genuine but puzzled, and she guessed he wanted to know who this young man was whose arm she was clutching.

And she wanted to tell him at once. 'Adam, I'd like you to meet Josh Harrison, he's going to join the practice as a registrar. I'm introducing him to people. Josh, Dr Fletcher is with us just for a few months, but he's making a definite impression.'

Josh shook the offered hand vigorously. 'Pleased to met you, sir. I've seen your programmes on TV, I think they're very sound. We were told to watch them in med school to learn how to talk to patients.'

Adam smiled. 'That's good to hear. And, please, Josh, it's Adam. Not sir.'

'Of course...Adam.'

'You'd better carry on with your introductions,' Adam went on to Lyn. 'I gather there's going to be dancing later. Save me a waltz?'

'My card shall be marked with your name. Now, come on, Josh. There'll be a test on all these names later.'

She thought she had handled that very well. Or perhaps Josh had handled it well.

The next person they met was Enid Sharpe, the district nurse who job-shared with Jane. It just so happened that she'd treated a much younger Josh, and could even remember him.

'You bent me over your knee and stuck a needle in my bottom,' Josh accused. 'However will you be able to treat me as a doctor with that in your mind?'

'I also remember you as a St John Ambulance cadet. I thought when I saw you working then that you'd the makings of a really good nurse. But you let me down and became a doctor. You'll enjoy it here.'

Lyn was enjoying herself now. She had met Adam, with no problems on either side. Later on perhaps she'd be able to join him. But for now...

Behind her there was a long fanfare. The band was starting to play and to considerable applause Jane and Cal took the floor first. After a while other couples joined them. Hesitantly, Josh said, 'Would you like to dance Lyn?' She agreed.

He was a good dancer and a pleasant young man. As they circled the floor she saw Adam looking her way and she thought—she hoped—he looked understanding. The second time she saw him he was dancing with Eunice Padgett.

They left the floor. Josh asked her if she'd like to dance again. 'Or is there someone you'd rather dance with?' he asked. 'Someone special?'

This was too accurate. 'No one at all,' she assured him, and they danced a second time. However, halfway through the dance they heard a female voice call, 'Good Lord, it's Josh—Josh Harrison. Josh, what are you doing here?'

They were confronted by a young couple who had known Josh at school. There seemed to be no point on carrying on dancing so they went in a group to the side of the floor where they met even more people. Apparently they all knew Josh from school days and were glad to see him rejoining them.

'You seem to be with a group now,' Lyn said to him, 'and you've met most of the practice members. I'll leave you to it, then.' And she slipped away. Perhaps she could have a dance—perhaps just one—

with Adam. She had seen him over by the far corner and...

'It's the gorgeous midwife Lyn! Come and dance with me, Lyn, and we'll see if we can win a spot prize.'

Before she could make her way over to where she thought Adam was, she was grabbed by Dr Jeff Standish. She knew Jeff quite well. He was the senior partner in a practice a few miles away and the two practices often worked together.

As usual on social occasions, Jeff was slightly drunk and entirely happy. They had a couple of noisy and not too unpleasant dances, and then Lyn was dragged back to the table where the rest of Jeff's practice was sitting. She was made very welcome there. Someone brought her a drink and she realised that if she wished she could spend the rest of the evening with the group.

It might be a good idea to stay with them. If she danced once with Adam then she'd want to dance again. Something in their body language was certain to alert other people. There'd be gossip and... She realised that she didn't care about the gossip. What was worse was the way she'd feel. She might weaken—as she had weakened on the cruiser. Yes, she'd keep her distance from Adam this way. It would hurt—but it was what was necessary.

She had a dance with another member of Jeff's group and when she returned she accepted another drink. Casually she glanced round the now full marquee. As expected, it was a successful party, it was easy to see that people were enjoying themselves.

And then she saw Adam. He was with a group, chatting politely, and she saw him glance her way.

Their eyes met. There was such misery in his expression that she knew at once what she had to do.

'I've been here long enough,' she said cheerfully. 'I must circulate. Hope to catch you all later.' And then, in spite of protests, she left and walked directly towards Adam.

She saw him looking at her as she approached, his face assessing, curious but half-pleased. He detached himself from the group and walked towards her so they could meet alone.

'I just had to come to you,' she said. 'I couldn't help myself and I'm sorry. I intended to keep a distance between us, but I can't and that's just terrible.'

'There's a table just outside,' he said. 'Come and sit down.'

There were other people in the garden so no one thought it strange that they should be, too. He led her to a garden seat, where they could sit in the moonlight, hear the music from the marquee but not be disturbed.

Under cover of the table he reached out and stroked her arm. She hadn't realised how such a simple caress could bring so much pleasure.

'You're with me now,' he said, 'and we have plenty of time. I want you to know that just sitting with you brings me so much pleasure. For now I don't want anything from you, no promises about the future, no plans about what we might do. I just want to be with you. Now, sit here for a while and, so that people won't talk, in a moment we'll go back inside and dance.'

'You're saying what I was telling myself. Why should I care what people think?'

'You care because they're your friends. Shall I fetch you a drink?'

'I'd rather you stayed here with me. We can get a drink in a minute.'

'As you wish.'

Lyn reached out and took his hand. No one could see now. And as she held it she wondered why she was so agitated. Probably it was because she knew she had caused him pain. And she, who had suffered so much pain, didn't want to cause it in anyone else.

'That new registrar, Josh Harrison, seems quite a pleasant chap,' Adam said. 'I think he should be an asset to the practice.'

It was what she wanted. A nice, safe, non-controversial topic. 'He's from round here originally,' she said. 'At the moment he's with a group of old friends. He's going to fit in well.'

'I heard he trained in Liverpool. I know a couple of people there, they're doing some good work on Alzheimer's.'

They talked further about medical matters and slowly her heart returned to its normal pace and she felt more at peace.

'I'd like to dance now,' she said. 'I want people to see my new dress and to see me with the best-looking man in the room.'

'Then you must dance with Cal. I've never seen a man look happier, and because he's happy he looks good.'

Lyn thought about that. 'I know what you mean. It's working for Jane, too. But right now it's you I want to dance with.'

So they danced. She should have known Adam would be an expert dancer. Or perhaps he wasn't expert, perhaps it was just that she found it so easy to guess how he was going to move next. Whatever it was, she loved being in his arms. And as they walked off the floor they were waylaid by Jane and Cal.

'He's going to make an honest woman of me at last,' Jane said cheerfully. 'Look, I've got my ring back. It's been at the jeweller's, being altered to fit me.' She showed it to them, bright, sparkling, on her left hand.

'It's beautiful,' said Lyn honestly, and then went on, she couldn't help herself, 'It's an antique, isn't it? A cabochon sapphire?'

She looked up to see Adam looking at her thoughtfully, and she knew he had picked up something from her tone. But happily neither Jane nor Cal had.

'That's right,' said Jane, 'and I love it.'

'So you'd recommend getting married?' Adam asked cheerfully.

'It's wonderful,' Jane said, 'I've opened a file on my computer and started planning already.'

'It's very hard work,' Cal said, and then added when Jane had playfully hit him, 'But I really enjoy it.'

Another couple came up to congratulate the pair, and Lyn and Adam walked away.

'Happy, aren't they?' Adam said. 'It makes me happy to look at them. And slightly envious, too. They knew what they wanted and they've both gone for it.'

'Are you trying to hint at something?'

He beamed at her. 'Would I do a thing like that? Certainly not. Let's join the queue and get something to eat.' So they did, taking plates of food to a table.

To Lyn's surprise she discovered that she was hungry. Perhaps emotion took energy and so she wanted to eat.

'You can tell me something if you want,' he said when they had both eaten enough, 'but you don't have to and I won't pry.'

'You can only ask,' said Lyn.

'When you saw Jane's ring. You knew at once that it was a cabochon sapphire. Is that the kind of thing that all women know?'

After a moment's silence she said, 'Some do, some don't. I knew because my engagement ring was a cabochon sapphire. The two are a little alike.' She lifted her hand, showed him her ring finger. 'I don't wear it now, it gets in the way. I just wear my wedding ring.'

'So you recognised the similarity.' His voice was gentle. 'It must have taken you back to a happier time. How did you feel?'

Lyn looked past him, out of the open marquee entrance to the darkened gardens beyond. Was this the time for complete honesty? Or should she pretend? That might be easier. But she found she couldn't deceive him.

'For nearly all of the past three years it would have upset me. It would have reminded me of Michael, of getting engaged to him, marrying him, living with him. The wonderful time we had together. But not now. It was good but now it has passed.'

Adam nodded. 'I think I see. So you were surprised yourself that you didn't feel so bad?'

'Yes, I was a bit surprised. But you have to look forward. There was a past, now there is a future. Though what it holds I don't know.'

He touched her arms again, she liked it. He said, 'You have your life in front of you and there's no need to hurry it. I hope that I can...can help in some way.'

She laughed. 'I think you've already done that. In what my old headmistress would call a very real fashion.' Then, even though it was dark, once again she blushed.

'A very enjoyable fashion,' he said. 'But you know you mean much more to me than that. It's quite a warm evening for this time of year, shall we go for a walk?'

'OK, just let me get my wrap.'

When she returned he took her arm and they strolled out of the marquee and into the garden. Others were doing the same as it was a hot night. But soon they were lost in the shrubbery and no one was near.

He stopped and put his arm round her waist, she rested her head on his shoulder. He felt big and warm and comforting. 'You've been honest with me,' he said. 'I'll be the same with you. When I thought you were deliberately ignoring me this evening, I felt worse than I'd ever felt in my life. No woman ever has affected me like you have. I just didn't know how I could cope. And it's not like me to admit to a weakness.'

'It's not a weakness,' she protested. 'It makes you a real, a more lovable person. I get fed up with these macho men who won't admit to their feelings. You think that if they don't show their feelings then perhaps they don't have them.'

'Possibly,' he said.

With a slight feeling of panic she realised she'd

talked herself into a corner. 'But there has to be some distance between us,' she said. 'We've agreed there has to be that.'

'No, we haven't. *You've* stipulated it, I've had to go along with it. And you still haven't told me why we have to keep apart. You must know that we...that I...have a regard for you.'

For a moment she was tempted to tell him about the letter. But she daren't. She knew what his instant reaction would be, knew that he would protest that it didn't matter. And she just could not rob him of the chance of having children.

So she temporised. 'I'm afraid,' she said.

He kissed her gently on the cheek. 'That's understandable,' he said. 'Let's go back to the party, enjoy the evening together and there'll be no more tough talking.'

Then she felt worse.

Lyn had arranged to stay the night at Cal's house as she was going to look after Helen and put her to bed. When they returned to the party Lyn looked out for her little charge, who was showing distinct signs of fatigue.

'I'm going to have to take this young lady away in ten minutes,' she told Adam, 'it's nearly bath-and bedtime for her. You don't mind do you?'

'Perhaps it's a good thing,' Adam said. 'But I do feel that things between us have progressed. We'll get there in the end.'

She didn't ask him what he'd meant by that. Perhaps it was a good thing if she didn't know.

CHAPTER EIGHT

HELEN had often stayed with Lyn in the past, and the two were old friends. Regretfully Lyn changed out of her red dress into a serviceable T-shirt and shorts and then bathed and read a story to the little girl. Helen had had a wonderful time and thought she would never get to sleep. But soon the little eyes closed and Lyn was left silent, sitting on the side of the bed.

She looked down at the perfect features, curled a strand of hair round her fingers. What was it really like to have, to bring up a baby? If she could feel this love for her friends' little girl, what would she have felt for a child of her own?

As a midwife she had learned to respond to the delight in a mother's face when first she saw her baby. It was one of the things that made being a midwife worthwhile, one of the joys of the job. Would she ever feel that joy herself?

Whenever it was possible, she liked to have the husband—or partner—present at the birth. It helped the mother, it made the father more fully a member of the family. And quite often there was joy on even the most hardened man's face when he saw his newborn child. She had seen tough farmers weep with happiness when she presented them with a scrap of humanity wrapped in a blanket.

She thought that Adam might weep, too. How could she deny him that happiness?

Lyn went to the window and peered out from behind the curtain. The party was ending now. She wondered if she might catch a glimpse of Adam, but he was nowhere to be seen. How she wished she could tell him everything, explain how she loved him but that they couldn't get married because she could never bear him the children he so much wanted. It just wasn't possible.

Lyn went straight to work next morning but when she dropped in at home at lunchtime there was a message on her answering machine. Emma, Adam's sister, had called. Emma sounded happy, carefree, said that this wasn't a serious message but could Lyn ring her back? Lyn wondered for a minute, then did so.

'How was last night?' Emma asked first. 'Adam's been talking about it for days. Anyone would think he'd never been to an engagement party before.'

'He was the best-looking man there,' Lyn said softly. 'We both had a wonderful time. In fact, everyone did.'

'I'm so glad. So you spent the evening with him?'

'Well, most of it.' Lyn was cautious.

'Good. We've been invited up to see the cottage and meet Cal and Jane. The kids are looking forward to it, but Adam says he's pretty busy right now and we'll come when things are a bit more settled.'

'Looking forward to seeing you,' said Lyn.

'Yes, me, too.' Lyn thought that Emma sounded hesitant, as if unsure what to say next. Then Emma went on, 'Look, Lyn, this isn't my business and Adam would be howling mad if he know I was interfering. But he's still my little brother. You know we were brought up in St Mark's?'

'Yes, he had told me.'

'Well, the staff did their best but when we first went there we just didn't know where our parents had gone and things were hard for us. I cried every night, Adam never would. It would have been good for him, 'cos he suffered so much and only I know it.'

'He was so lucky to have you,' Lyn said, her voice hoarse.

'We had each other. We got through things and now we're happy.'

Lyn thought she could hear a tremor in Emma's voice. Emma went on, 'Adam phones us a couple of times a week and we chat about this and that. He sounds happy, he's now a doctor, a big man, confident in what he does and really enjoying this new job. But when he talks to me sometimes I think I can hear that little boy's voice again. He's hurting.'

Lyn leaned back in her chair and in desperation rubbed her forehead with her free hand. She didn't know what to say. 'I...I like him a lot,' she mumbled. 'We get on well together, there's no man I'd rather...but I'm worried that...Emma, I wouldn't deliberately cause him pain!'

'I know that, Lyn,' Emma said gently. 'You're obviously a nice person. We all thought Adam was so lucky when he brought you to see us. I just wanted to let you know that if there's any way I can help, then I will. Hope to see you soon and the kids send their love. Bye.' And she rang off.

Lyn sat there, unable to move. Emma's words had hurt her more than she liked to admit. The thought of the suffering of that little boy—he must carry it still with him. Had she been unfair to him? But she couldn't think of anything she could do.

There was one small thing. Before she set off on

her afternoon rounds she scribbled a quick note and put it through his letter-box. 'Help! There was so much food left last night that Jane gave me a great box of it. Please come and help me get through some of it. A meal of leftovers after you've finished evening surgery? Love, Lyn.' That should do it.

'Not a date or an assignation or anything like that,' she said when Adam presented himself at her door in the evening. 'Just a couple of friends eating up some scraps and then enjoying each other's company.'

'Sounds good to me. And just in case, I brought a bottle of wine.' He followed her into her kitchen and stared at the vast number of plates. 'Did you say eating up some scraps?'

'That was Jane's phrase. I didn't think it was a particularly accurate one. Now, let's sit down and start.'

He seemed to recognize her mood and reacted to it. For the moment they forgot themselves and talked about their work. He was getting very interested in the outreach clinic and told her how useful it was to some of the outlying farms.

'You're getting to sound like one of the locals,' she said playfully.

He took her seriously. 'I'd like to be one.'

They washed up together and then sat together on her couch. Since Lyn was technically on call, she refused a glass of wine but insisted that he have one.

Adam put his arm round her shoulders and she nestled into his chest. 'Right now I'm happy,' she told him. 'I don't want to think, I don't want to talk, I don't want to plan. I just want to be here with you. The future doesn't exist. There's only now.'

He kissed her forehead. 'I'm happy, too, Lyn,' he said. And there they stayed, quiet, contented. And at eight o'clock Lyn's mobile rang.

The voice on the other end was sheepish. 'I'm sorry to bother you, Lyn. I thought this was a false alarm, but the contractions got more and more frequent, and now the waters have broken. I'm properly in labour.'

Lyn had known Frances Lane for years. She was a calm, capable farmer's wife with two sons already. Frances had had a scan, and knew that her third child was to be a girl. She was looking forward to having a daughter.

The baby was due in a fortnight. Frances had done everything correctly, had been to all the classes Lyn had run, was in all ways prepared. Her previous two children had been born at exactly the predicted time. She had discussed it with Lyn and had decided to have this baby at home.

'You're early,' Lyn said. This was the last thing she had expected—in fact, the last thing she needed. Years of experience should have told her that babies had minds of their own.

'I know I'm early, and you've probably got things you have to do. Do you want me to phone an ambulance? Or is there another district midwife?'

Lyn glanced at her watch. To her amazement it was only eight o'clock. She'd had a full day. 'I'm on my way, Frances,' she said firmly. 'I should be there in about half an hour. Just try to relax. You know the exercises we practiced.'

Then she turned to Adam. 'This has happened before,' she said. 'Just like it did with Hetty Summers.'

'Then your patient can have a midwife and a doctor. Just as Hetty did.'

'There's no need. You must be tired and this could take hours. Why don't you—?'

'And I remember what happened when we came back from helping Hetty Summers.'

'Adam!'

He held up his hands. 'I'm only joking. We have work to do now, let's do it. I'll fetch my bag from next door and we'll be off. Want to let the surgery know where we are?'

'As always, I'll leave a message. Now, I've got five minutes to get into a clean uniform.'

They took her car as it was her call-out. The farm wasn't too far away and they were met by Alan, Frances's husband, who was as calm as she was.

'Frances's ma had taken the kids,' he said. 'We're all prepared, but if you want Frances to go to hospital then we'll go along with that.'

'Let's see how things are progressing first,' Lyn said. 'This is Dr Fletcher. He's here as—'

'I'm here as a makeweight,' Adam said. 'Lyn will do the delivery.'

Lyn went up to see Frances, looked at the carefully set-out room, the cot waiting in readiness. Next door was the bathroom, very handy.

First, a quick examination and then the inevitable paperwork. Lyn chatted to the relaxed and confident Frances as the labour took its natural course. This was how home births ought to be, Lyn thought. Frances had worked hard on her relaxation exercises and said that she needed no pain relief. All was going well. As always, Lyn felt involved in the process, her previous fatigue now forgotten. Adam came in, was introduced to Frances and then said he would wait outside. He was there if needed.

The baby would be born soon. Frances's face took on that expression of excitement and fear that Lyn knew so well. The head had crowned. 'All right, you can push now,' Lyn urged. Frances grimaced, and pushed.

She pushed well, but after fifteen minutes there was no further progress, and after twenty minutes Lyn was slightly worried. Frances was now showing signs of weariness. Something wasn't quite right.

Cautiously, Lyn felt past the baby's head and knew instantly what the trouble was. The baby was stuck, the shoulders not rotating into the position for an easy birth.

'I think we'll ask Dr Fletcher in,' she said to Frances, 'just to have his opinion on things.' She kept her voice calm, there was no need to frighten the patient.

She went into the next room and shut the door behind her. 'Adam, we have a case of shoulder distochia.'

Adam was instantly alert. 'Has she had an episiotomy?'

'No. So far it hasn't seemed necessary.'

'I'll go and scrub up. Make sure Frances had plenty of gas and air, get her into the McRoberts position and perform an episiotomy. Then we'll see how things are going. Send Alan out. I'll tell him to phone for an ambulance. We might need hospital help.'

'Right.' Lyn returned to her patient. 'Just a little problem Frances,' she said, 'Dr Fletcher is coming in to give me a hand. And we think we'd like you to go to hospital to be checked over.'

'I'll have my baby here first?' Frances was anxious.

'I'm sure you will. Now, I want you to lie on your

back and pull your thighs up and outwards. You need an episiotomy so I'm going to give you an injection, which might sting a little. And I want you to start using the gas and air.'

It was a straightforward procedure but she was glad when Adam appeared by her side and smiled down at the troubled Frances. 'Your baby won't turn round,' he explained gently, 'and she needs to, in order to be born. I'm going to push down here to try and dislodge the shoulder and ease her round. It's called applying suprapubic pressure. Now, I don't want you to worry.'

Somehow Frances managed to smile. 'I've seen Alan pull a calf out with a rope round its neck,' she said, 'and both calf and cow were fine. So I guess I can take a bit of pressure.'

He pressed—but the baby didn't move. Lyn looked at him, still apparently calm and smiling, but could sense the urgency he was feeling. From being an ordinary birth, this was turning into a nightmare.

Without saying anything, he moved away from the side of Frances, positioned himself between her legs and reached into the birth canal, trying to rotate the shoulders though 180 degrees so that the posterior shoulder was anterior. He didn't succeed. And now the baby's life was in danger.

There was one last thing to try. 'I'm going to see if I can deliver the posterior arm,' he said. 'I need to get my hand into the sacrum, get hold of the arm, pull it over the chest and get the hand out. Then there should be no difficulty in delivering the arms and then the baby.'

'Of course,' she said. It was something she had never done, a manoeuvre usually performed by a gynaecologist in Theatre with a team of assistants. A farmhouse bedroom wasn't the right place.

She looked at Adam. He was maintaining the usual medical calm, but she could tell by the slight dampness on his upper lip, the slightly deeper tone of his voice that he was nervous. He knew what a risk he was taking, what the possible consequences were.

'This shouldn't take a minute,' he said to Frances. And behind her patient, Lyn squeezed her eyes shut in a moment's silent prayer. She knew what failure would mean to Frances—and to Adam.

She watched Adam's intent face as he reached for the tiny arms and tried to manoeuvre the now distressed baby. And then, slowly, he smiled. He had done it. He stepped back and said, 'All should be as normal now. You deliver the baby, I'll stay here and take it.'

He leaned over Frances and smiled. 'Panic over now, Frances. We'll have the baby out very soon now.'

'I knew I didn't have to worry,' Frances muttered. Lyn wondered if she could see the expression of joy and relief on Adam's face.

After that, all went according to plan. Adam was hardly needed. Soon they had a fine, yelling baby girl. Lyn weighed her, cleaned her, went through the usual necessary tests, wrote up the Apgar score and placed her on her mother's breast. The placenta was delivered normally.

Shortly after that the ambulance arrived, and they decided to send mother and child to hospital just in case. 'But it was a home birth,' Frances said. 'Thank you so much, both of you.'

'We both enjoyed it,' Adam said.

* * *

Past midnight again when they got back to her house, Lyn didn't even need to ask Adam if he was coming in. He flopped onto her couch.

'You've been through more than me this evening,' she said flatly. 'You were worried in case you failed.'

'It was a nightmare. Just one of those things that happen. But we managed, Lyn, didn't we? We managed. And she was a lovely baby.'

'You managed. I think it was one of the bravest things I've ever seen anyone do. Now I'll fetch us a drink.'

They sat side by side, her head on his shoulder, his arm loosely round her. Perhaps later they would go to bed, but now they were content just to be together.

'Just having you here makes me feel calm and cosy.' The words came out before Lyn could stop herself.

He didn't reply and after a moment she started to worry. His body had been relaxed but now it tensed. He turned his head from side to side and she had the feeling that he was searching for words, trying to say something that was precisely right.

Eventually he said, 'This evening we went through something together. We were a team, each knew what the other needed. Now we need to be a team again. Lyn, tell my why you won't let me say I love you.'

She jerked upright. 'Please, Adam, not now. I'm tired and I—'

'If not now then when? We'll never be more together than we are at this minute! Lyn, this is…this is a barrier between us and it's driving me mad! I know you love me. And I can't imagine anything so terrible that you can't tell me.'

'You can't imagine,' she said desolately. 'And you think you want to know?'

A tiny part of her mind protested that this wasn't fair, he had asked her when she was weak, vulnerable. Another part of her desperately wanted to tell him, to share her secret.

'I need to know,' he said. He looked at her assessingly. 'You're going to tell me. And I'll love you just as much when you have told me as I do now. That I know, and that I promise you.'

'I know you will,' she said. 'But it's not enough.'

She forced herself to move a little away from him, to stare stony-eyed at the wall opposite. 'Just tell me what you see as our ideal life together. How you might see us in ten years—if we were still together.'

She could tell he was picking his words with infinite care.

'First, there's no rush. We need time to get to know each other better, to settle into each other's lives. And that should be fun. But then I see me staying, working up here, having a home together, being with friends, having children.'

'How many children?'

'We'd both decide after you've had the first. But three...I'd like four children.'

'How about no children?'

He laughed. 'Lyn, you love children! I've seen you with the newborns, with Helen, with lots of others. You were born to be a mother.'

'It's a pity, then, that I can't have them.'

'What?'

Never had she heard such disbelief, such horror in a voice. She turned to look at him. 'I checked with the consultant. After I had that miscarriage there was so much scarring, there's no chance of my conceiving. Adam, I can't have children.'

'Oh, my love!' He took her to him, kissed the tears now running down her face. 'Look, it doesn't matter. We have each other and we can—'

She stopped him. 'I know what you're going to say and I believe you mean it. But, please, Adam, I want you to be honest with me. Two choices—one, living with me and our children, two, living with me and no children. Which would make you happier?'

'That's not fair! I love you and we can sort things—'

'I want an answer, Adam! Adam, tell me! And be honest, I deserve that.'

It took an age before he replied. His face was haunted, there was even the steely glitter of a tear in his eye. She could tell the struggle he was having. And eventually he muttered, 'I've always wanted children. But, Lyn—'

'If I can't give you children,' she said, 'I'll never marry you. And no argument will make me change my mind. Now, I dearly want you to stay the night, but I think you'd better go.'

CHAPTER NINE

NORMALLY Adam slept from the moment his head hit the pillow to five minutes before he was due to rise. This time he thought that he'd stay awake for ever when he got into bed. But his overtaxed brain had had enough and he slept at once.

In the morning he woke an hour early, and he knew that he wouldn't go back to sleep. What could he do about Lyn? His first reaction was the same as it had been the night before—he didn't care whether she could have children or not. He loved her. But then his native honesty took over. He did love children.

And then his phone rang. He looked at it gloomily. For a doctor an unexpected early morning call was usually bad news. He knew it wouldn't be Lyn, she'd just ring his doorbell. Not that there was much chance of it. He picked up the phone.

'I'm ringing you early because I just have to talk to you,' a voice said. 'And this is important.'

'Ros? I thought we'd got things settled for a while, put the programmes on hold. I'm supposed to be taking it easy for six months—being a country doctor.'

'So you are and so you can be for the rest of the six months. But something has come up. We've had a query from America. A company out there has seen your work and wants to know if we're interested in running a series together. We'd be selling to the British and the American markets. This would be fantastic—and mean a tremendous increase in the amount you earn.'

'I like the idea of working and making a programme at the same time. But it's in America.'

'Adam,' Ros pleaded, 'this could be the big chance for both of us. Will you at least come and talk to these people?'

He thought. Ros had been good to him, perhaps he owed her this chance. But was he sure himself?

'It's early and it's a bit of a shock, Ros,' he said. 'Let me think about it for a couple of days.'

Her voice was plaintive. 'Think about it, Adam. You'd be so good at it.' Then she rang off. She knew that pushing him too hard usually wasn't successful.

He lay in bed, wondering. Since he'd come to Keldale, he'd hardly missed working in television. Now he had other interests. And after last night's revelation it seemed supremely unimportant.

He went downstairs, made himself a drink and sat holding it in his living room. He was conscious that not ten feet away, on the other side of the wall, Lyn might be doing the same as he was. She had told him that sometimes she thought of him in this way. It seemed odd to him.

Last night had been traumatic—for both of them. Now he just didn't know what to do. His first reaction was still to storm next door and tell her that having children didn't matter. He loved her. But he knew that there was a strength of mind in her that wouldn't be easily swayed. Reluctantly, he realized that they both needed time. And then perhaps he could approach her again.

Adam had a good morning at the surgery and then a list of home visits to make in the afternoon. He didn't see Lyn, who was out herself, making home visits.

It was yet another glorious day. The sun had that deep orange tint that only comes with autumn, the leaves were turning russet brown. This year the change had come early.

He was calling on Albert Dent, a fifty-five-year-old farmer who owned a prosperous farm in the river valley. A few weeks ago Albert had slipped from the top of a hayrick, suffering a compound fracture of both tibia and fibula. Complications had set in, the leg had taken time to mend and now Adam knew he wasn't bringing good news.

He spread the X-rays he had brought on the table. 'I wanted to show you exactly what the trouble is, Albert,' he said. 'Your leg was fractured here and here. The orthopedic surgeon pinned it, did the best he could. I know you've been having physiotherapy for the past few weeks, and the therapist says you've done your exercises religiously. You've even lost a few pounds, which can't be bad. But...'

'But I'll never be as good as I was,' Albert said sadly. 'I'll never be able to walk all day without some pain, never be able to carry the loads I carried before.'

'It's not all bad news. If you take care of yourself you should be fine. But before you were working harder than a twenty-year-old should have to work. Now you can carry on working—but you must take it easier.'

'And if I don't?'

'The pain will make sure that you do,' Adam told him bluntly. 'And if you don't listen to your body you could end up in a wheelchair.'

Albert nodded. He limped over to the window and

gazed out at his fields, and the fells beyond them. 'I guess I was expecting you to say something like that. But it'll be hard to sit here when there's things to be done. I've worked this farm since I was seven.'

Adam had got to know the farmer quite well and the two men got on together. 'Your wife died three years ago, Albert,' he said. 'You've a son in the next valley who could take over here just as you took over from your father. The farm would be in good hands. Another generation of Dents.'

'My father took it hard, having to hand over.' Albert was silent a minute, then turned and said decisively, 'I know you're right and I know I can't go on like this. I'll hand the farm over. But I'm not staying here. You know I've another son, farms in New Zealand? He and his wife have been on at me for ages, asking me to go over and live with them. They say they'd find a job for me, just enough to keep me occupied. And I could see more of my grandchildren.'

'It sounds good, but don't hurry decisions,' Adam said cautiously. 'You have to think about things first.'

'Something's got to be done so I'm going to do it quickly. The time comes when it's foolish to put off decisions, no matter how painful they might be. I'll miss Larkcall Farm, but I'm going.'

'Perhaps you're right,' Adam said.

The road from Larkcall Farm ran up the side of the fell, curved round a rocky outcrop and dropped into the next valley, where it met the main road. There was a place to pull off at the curve at the top, and Adam parked and went to sit on the grass. In front of him was the valley, a patchwork of fields. The steep hills on either side weren't cultivated, but sheep grazed on the rough pasture. In the distance he could just see the sea. It was a peaceful landscape, beautiful and very British.

Adam thought about the man he had just spoken to, the decision he had made. *The time comes when it's foolish to put off decisions, no matter how painful they might be.* Instinctively, Adam knew that Albert was right.

He had to make a decision over Lyn. He had to get her to offer him some hope, no matter how little. He had to be able to think that some day they might be...well, much closer. He couldn't stand this uncertainty. Soon there would be the time, the opportunity, and he would do it. And if Lyn turned him down—then he would lose himself in work, as so often he had done before. Work with Ros in America. Not entirely satisfied with what he had decided, Adam went back to his car.

'I really enjoyed the party,' Joanne Morris said to Lyn the next day. 'It was good, wasn't it?' She stood up from the examination couch. 'Is everything all right?'

Joanne's voice was over-casual, and Lyn knew that she was worried. That was the trouble with doctors and nurses as patients—they always knew too much, had their own opinions. And, of course, they could never be dispassionate.

Joanne was a junior doctor, one of the registrars at the practice. She was six months pregnant and had come to Lyn with a slightly raised blood pressure.

'Well, as you know, this isn't exactly normal,' Lyn said. 'But I suspect it's got worse because you've been worrying about it, haven't you? You know taking your own BP is, well, not always a good idea.'

Joanne looked embarrassed. 'It's hard not to,' she

mumbled. 'And I know I'm not an older mum, but I am a bit overweight.'

'So you took your own BP and instantly thought pre-eclampsia!'

'Well, yes.'

Lyn smiled. It was hard not to feel sympathy. She remembered how she herself had been alert for any possible problem when she'd been pregnant. 'Probably nothing to worry about,' she said, 'but what I'd like to do is get one of the doctors to have a quick look at you. Any feelings about which one you'd like?'

As Joanne was a member of the practice, it was possible to bend the rules a little for her. She could pick her own doctor.

'Dr Fletcher if possible. He's the one I know least well.' A very understandable reaction.

It was late in the morning and the doctors usually reserved this time to answer telephone queries. Lyn checked with the receptionist and Adam was available. She put her head round his door and said, 'If you've got a moment, I could do with a bit of professional advice. In my examination room?'

She didn't tell him who it was or what the problem was. She didn't want Joanne thinking that she'd talked behind her back.

Lyn sat, watched and listened. She thought Adam was good with Joanne. At first he made no move to examine his patient. Instead, he chatted about her training, talked about what her future might be. Only when she was thoroughly relaxed did he access her details on the computer and then ask her what was worrying her. 'My blood pressure's too high. And I thought—'

He laughed. 'I can guess. Pre-eclampsia. Thoroughly understandable. I'd think the same thing if I were pregnant and a doctor. Well, let's have a look at you.'

And the now relaxed Joanne had no difficulty with the examination at all.

'What do you think, Midwife Pierce?' Adam asked cheerfully. 'Diagnosis and treatment, please? You once told me you'd seen far more births than I ever had.'

'You're the doctor. But I suspect that all that is necessary is bed rest. At home will be fine. But we'll monitor progress and if necessary send her to hospital.'

'I agree. No drugs at all?'

'At the moment, no. Joanne should stop work at once for at least two weeks. Plenty of time in bed, no heavy work at all, minimum of physical exercise. At the end of that time we look at her again.'

'Hang on, I work here,' Joanne protested. 'I'm only six months gone, we've planned it that I work for another eight weeks. The practice needs me.'

'We do need you,' Adam said gently. 'If you go now, there's going to be more work for the rest of us. This is your decision but you've got to think of the baby. Now I suggest you have a word with your husband, perhaps have a word with Cal and then make up your mind. You can carry on with your training when you've had your baby. There's your life ahead of you.'

Joanne was silent a moment, then said, 'I suppose you're right. Now, I've got some visits this afternoon but tomorrow I could—'

'Go and see Cal,' Adam said. 'Don't tell him you

feel fine and you can carry on—it's not true. And he won't believe you anyway. Tell him what's wrong and then go home.'

'But I—'

'What would you say to a young woman who came to you as a doctor, with what's wrong with you? If you say anything other than what I've said, then you need more training.'

'I suppose you're right. I'll go and see Cal now.'

Adam and Lyn were left facing each other. It was a week since she told him her secret. When he'd gone home the next evening, after Albert Dent, he had found a note in his letter-box. 'We both need time to think. How about a few days when we don't see each other alone? And Adam, I *do* care for you. Lyn.'

He had thought for an hour before writing back. 'If you think that is best. But remember, I love you and I'm here for you. Adam.'

Now she looked at him uncertainly. But he seemed to be sticking to their unwritten truce. He said, 'Nearly all the mums I see now look to be little more than children. And the dads are the same. It makes me feel old. Time is slipping by me.'

'Rubbish,' Lyn said. 'There's plenty of years in you yet. You're not old.'

But she wondered why he had made the half-comic remark. Was there a hint there? Time was passing for everyone.

At lunchtime next day Lyn managed to call in at home again, and as she stood at the front door Ros's dark green car pulled up. Ros opened the car window and smiled at Lyn. 'Is there any point in trying to have a quick word with Adam? It's not urgent and I know he hates it when I disturb him at work.'

Lyn thought of the surgery she had just left, and sighed. 'At the moment we're bursting. All the doctors are frantic. Adam won't be free for at least another hour.'

'That bad? Well, I can't wait. I've got to drive down to London now so I'll phone him this evening.'

'Come and have a cup of tea first.'

'I'd like that,' Ros said. 'I'm glad I caught you. I've got something for you.'

As they sat drinking tea she handed Lyn a small packet. 'I haven't forgotten how you patched my hand when we first met. This is a tiny present from me to say thank you.'

'But I didn't—'

'Please!' said Ros. 'It's just a small something.'

Lyn opened the packet. Inside was a dark green leather box containing a pair of earrings. Lyn took them out, fascinated. She'd never had anything like them before. Normally all she wore were plain gold studs. But these were different, drop earrings in a barbaric pattern of silver and turquoise. She went to her mirror and put them on.

'Let me see,' Ros said. 'I know what works visually.'

Lyn turned and Ros went on with some satisfaction, 'I knew you'd look good in those. It's that heart-shaped face, those good cheekbones. Not every woman could wear them—I certainly wouldn't dare to. But you can.'

Lyn felt complimented, the more so because Ros had been so detached in her assessment. She realised she was coming out of her shell. For so long she hadn't cared if she was complimented, now she thought she liked it.

'Thank you so much. They're lovely,' she said. 'Now I'm going to look for a chance to wear them. But tell me, what's this problem with Adam?'

Ros looked exasperated. 'I love that man but he can be so irritating! He's changing! Or this countryside is changing him! The idea was that he should come here for just six months, have a kind of sabbatical, get back to his roots as a doctor. Then back to the city, medicine there and more TV work with me. And I've had an offer from an American firm that could be really big! But now he's talking about staying here indefinitely. Any idea why?'

Lyn shrugged. 'Not really,' she said.

Ros seemed suddenly to have a new idea. She looked at Lyn shrewdly. 'It's not you, is it?'

Lyn thought she managed to look calm. 'Not at all,' she said with a laugh. 'I'm a widow. I've been in love and I just don't want another relationship.'

'Hmm,' Ros said, and Lyn hoped she had been believed. Ros went on, 'Adam could be big and that would mean that I would get to be big with him. But I've got a lot of regard for him as a friend—I suppose I love the old grouse. I want him to be happy. If staying round here makes him happy, then good luck to him. I'll support him.'

She put down her cup and stood. 'I'd better be off. Tell him I called. I'll phone him later. And wear the earrings. They look good!' Then she was gone.

Lyn went back to the mirror and looked at herself. Yes, the earrings did look good. But the news she had just heard wasn't so good.

She just couldn't manage to keep away from

Adam. If he was around, then she would be drawn to him. They were drawn to each other. The slightest misery in his face made her soul ache.

He had come for six months and so far he had been here about two. Perhaps she could manage to maintain a brave face for another four months. But if he stayed here indefinitely? Living next door to her? She just couldn't manage that. The pain would be too much. She might have to think about leaving.

CHAPTER TEN

IT HAD been the best summer and autumn that people could remember. The warm unseasonal weather continued, every night there seemed to be a programme pointing out that Britain now had the best weather in Europe and considering the prospect of global warming. It was hot, it was dry, it was wonderful.

Lyn loved it. But being close to the land, she knew that the continued lack of rain wasn't a good thing. The farmers were complaining—complaining of a lack of water in the rainy Lake District!

And after a while there was a new threat—forest fires. There were outbreaks all over, often in the plantations of easily combustible fir trees.

Lyn set off the next afternoon to visit yet another of her patients who lived on the very outskirts of her area, travelling through yet another maze of tiny back roads. After a while there was the roar of engines behind her and sound of a siren wailing. She pulled into a field entrance and let three great fire engines pass. Over the past few days she had seen several of them. The crews were working almost non-stop.

It was Martha Evans's third baby, the birth had been smooth and everything was all right. Martha was an experienced and intelligent mother. Lyn had, of course to make a number of statutory calls, but she knew there would be absolutely no need for her inspection. Still, she called, had an iced drink and saw that all was fine.

She set off for home. Her car had been in the sun, and it was quite warm inside. Lyn pulled her uniform away from her body, wiped her face. Perhaps when she started driving the draft would cool her.

As she drove on she felt the car rock. The wind was growing stronger and she saw trees bending as the breeze increased. She shuddered. Fire, humidity and wind were an evil combination. She hoped there would be no more trouble.

She was driving past a small plantation near the top of a hill when she saw a car parked by the side of the road. She squinted. Surely that was Adam's car? As she thought that he appeared and waved to her to pull in behind him. She did. What was Adam doing out here?

He came to her open window, his expression for once stern. 'I knew you'd come back this way,' he said. 'I saw you were booked in to visit Martha Evans.'

Some of the areas the staff visited were wild and lonely. It was one of Cal's rules that all staff making visits should log in where they were going and roughly when they expected to arrive and leave.

'You could have phoned me on my mobile if you wanted to meet me. What's so important?'

'We have to talk. And I wanted to do it well away from the surgery, from our houses even.'

'But why now? And why no warning?'

'Now, because I can't go on any longer like this. And no warning because I think we need to approach things without time to prepare. We need instant honesty.'

For the first time his face showed signs of uncertainty. 'We need to sort things out, Lyn. Can you spare half an hour to talk to me?'

'All afternoon if you want,' she said. 'If you're sure it's a good idea.'

'You don't think it is?'

'I don't know,' she said sadly, 'I don't know what you're going to say.' But she had a good idea, and she wasn't looking forward to it.

They drove their cars into the trees, and then he led her through the plantation along a broad path. She knew where they were going—in half a mile there was a plateau where they could survey the full length of Lake Windermere and see the Langdales beyond.

He offered her his hand, she took it. And they walked in silence.

Finally they reached the plateau. For a moment they looked at the view, but it wasn't as clear as it should have been. Here and there they could see a thick haze which Lyn knew to be smoke. There were fires raging, or fires under control. They desperately needed rain.

There was a log to sit on, they sat side by side. She had said nothing so far, she wanted him to start the conversation, to lead it. She was frightened about where it might go.

'I'm supposed to be a communicator,' he said, 'supposed to be good with words. I've tried to rehearse this speech and I've got nowhere. I think I know what I want to say but I'm scared of saying it.'

'Why not wait, then?' she asked in a small voice. 'Think about things a bit more?' She didn't want him to speak. She thought that whatever he said would result in her having to make some kind of decision, and she didn't want to decide anything. And decisions once made were hard to reverse.

'I don't want to wait! In fact, I can't wait! Do you know what you're doing to me, Lyn, what it's like being so close to you and yet having to keep my distance? It hurts!'

'I think I know what it's like. In fact, I do know. And, Adam, the last thing I want to do is hurt you. I'd rather hurt myself.'

He was silent now and leaned towards her. She hoped he wouldn't kiss her, it would make things so much harder.

'We want no talk of hurting,' he said. Then he moved to the end of the log, sat well away from her.

'There's something between us,' he said. 'It started the first time we met, when you capsized. It started the minute you opened your eyes. I don't know what it is, but I've never felt it before, and you feel it, too. Don't you?'

Her lips were dry but she managed to mutter, 'Well, I know what you're talking about.'

'No! You feel it, Lyn!'

She had to be honest. 'Yes, I feel it. I've said so before. But that's not to say that things aren't... awkward.'

'We can deal with awkward. Now, you've said I mustn't use the word "love" so I won't. But I will say I'm getting more and more...fond of you.' His lips twisted as he said the word. 'I've never felt anything like this before. And because it's been so long coming, I think it's so much stronger. Now I want you to tell me you feel the same. Not right now, I can wait. I'll wait days, weeks, months just so long as I know I'll get an answer one day.'

Adam stopped. There was nothing she could say, this was all too much. What was worst was that she knew he was telling the truth.

He went on, 'The last thing I want to do is hurt you, but I feel that you owe me something. Now, I'm going for a walk for five minutes to give you time get your thoughts together. You say you can't have babies and because of this you won't consider a long-term relationship with me. Lyn, I've thought about this a lot. Whatever happens, I want to be with you. But if you feel you can't be with me, then I'll respect that and leave you alone. In fact, I'll leave the practice. I've had a quiet word with Cal, told him about that offer of more TV work in America. He says that it would be awkward but he could release me from my contract.'

This was something she could seize on. 'See? We lead different lives! I don't want to go to live in London—or America!'

He smiled. 'I don't believe that. Or perhaps it's not important. One, I'd rather live here. Two, I know you. If you were in love and it was necessary, then you'd follow your lover anywhere. But now I'm going for my five minutes. Then I want an answer.'

He stretched his hand along the log, took hold of hers. 'Just to calm things down a bit, I had a phone call from my sister this morning asking both of us go to John's birthday party next week. I said I'd let her know.' Then he stood and walked till he was out of sight.

Lyn didn't know whether to laugh or cry. He didn't know it but his last remark had been the clincher. She had been wavering—perhaps she could tell him, perhaps all would be well, they could sort things out.

But his delight at the prospect of seeing his sister's children was so great. How could she deny a man like this the chance of his own family?

She didn't have to think any further. She sat there, letting the tears run down her cheeks. She would tell him there could be nothing between them. He was to go back to London, follow his career.

She heard the crackle of footsteps. He was returning, but she didn't look up. Only when he was directly in front of her did she look up at that wonderful face. She said nothing but guessed he could read her expression. Certainly, she could read his. There had been hope, a little smile. But as she gazed at him she saw the smile disappear, to be followed by great sadness. Then there was the bleakness of acceptance.

Still no word had been said. She would have to tell him, she owed him that. Around them the hot wind grew stronger, shaking the trees. But she would have to tell him.

She opened her mouth—and it happened again. His mobile rang.

He muttered something but he answered it. And as he listened she saw his face change, become alert. Then he looked strained, angry almost. This was not about them any more, this was something else.

She found she could speak to him now. 'Adam, what is it?'

He took her hand, pulled her upright and hurried her down the path, back towards the cars. 'How far are we from Laddenside Forest? The east entrance from the Theakstone Road?'

She considered. She knew the area, he didn't. 'About two miles. We could be there in five minutes. Why?'

'There's a forest fire there, a bad one. They have three appliances fighting it and there are casualties. They need at least one doctor. They radioed to ask if anyone was handy. Eunice picked up the call and remembered I was out this way. If you can show me the way there then you can go and—'

'No. I'm coming, too. If they need a doctor then they could do with a nurse. And that's me.'

'But it could be dangerous! Lyn, I don't want you—'

'Adam! This isn't a decision you can make for me! I'm coming and that's final. Now, follow me. We'll be there quite quickly.'

By now they were both trotting along the path, sweat breaking out all over their bodies.

They came to their cars, opened all the windows and set off at once. She worked out the route and led him through the tangled little roads towards the east entrance of Laddenside Forest.

After she had travelled a mile a new smell came into the car through the open windows. It was acrid, unpleasant, the smell of something burning. And the wind was growing stronger, buffeting the car. She remembered that the combination of wind and fire was a deadly one.

Eventually they turned into the east entrance. There was a barrier across it and a policeman there waved them down. 'Sorry, ma'am, I'll have to ask you to go back to the main road. We have an emergency here, a forest fire.'

'I'm a nurse and the man behind me is a doctor. We're needed and we're expected.'

The policeman saw her uniform, opened the barrier and waved her through.

She bounced along the path, conscious of Adam's car close behind her. Both were driving vehicles suited for this kind of terrain.

It was hot! And the air was thick, hazy. It was hard to breathe. White ash danced in it. Now she knew they were close to a fire. She could even hear a distant crackling. The flames must be quite close.

They turned into a clearing and she realised that this must be some kind of a command post. There was a giant red appliance there. To the side of it there was an awning and there were bodies lying under it.

A fireman ran up to them. 'This is a danger area, we've no time for tourists so will you turn round and—?'

Adam got out of his car. 'We're a doctor and nurse,' he called firmly. 'We were sent for. Now, who do we report to?'

'Sorry,' said the fireman as he looked at them properly. 'Have a word with Jack Leonard over there. He's Divisional Officer, in charge.' He pointed to a man bending over one of the bodies under the awning.

'I'm glad you're here,' Jack Leonard said, briskly shaking hands. 'If you can do what you can for our injured, it'll free up another two men for firefighting.'

'You have sent for ambulances?' Adam asked.

'I've sent for them. But there are three other fires, each with injured, and so we have to wait our turn. The ambulance service is stretched pretty thin.'

He looked at the bags that both Lyn and Adam were carrying. 'For the past couple of weeks we've been carrying a pretty good medical box ourselves but I've no idea what most of the things in it are supposed to do. We usually just call an ambulance but, as I said, they're stretched thinner than we are.' He pointed to the awning. 'The box is there. Now, I'm going to leave you to it. Call for me if there's anything you need.'

'Seems a good man,' Adam muttered. 'Let's see what we've got here.'

He beckoned to one of the firemen who had been tending the injured and led him out of earshot of those lying still. 'Tell me what you've got,' he said, 'I know you all get some medical training so you must have some idea.'

The fireman obviously was pleased at being consulted. 'A set of forestry workers were trying to fight the fire and left it too late before pulling out. Should have left it to us. Anyway, they were in a lorry, moving too fast, and it overturned. We got there just in time. Everyone's a bit bruised and cut. All suffering from smoke inhalation, but not too badly. Two men badly burned, not life-threatening but in pain. One of the others seemed to be all right at first but he seems to be having difficulty breathing now. Perhaps his chest is bruised. All we've managed to do so far is make sure nobody is actually dying.'

'Was it only wood-smoke?' Lyn asked. 'No chemicals or anything like that burning?'

The fireman looked at her with respect. 'Just wood-smoke,' he said.

'This man with the difficulty breathing—was he trapped at all?' Adam asked.

The fireman nodded. 'The driver. He was thrown out of the cab, the mirror was pressing into him. We managed to prise it off.' He handed Adam a piece of paper. 'These are the names and what we've noticed so far.'

'This is excellent! You've done a really good job.

We'll take over now.' He turned to Lyn. 'You said you've worked in A and E? D'you want to check the two burned and the smoke inhalations? See if anything's been missed, try and make them comfortable. I'll look at this crushed chest.'

'OK. I'll call if I need you.' This was work totally different from the midwifery that had occupied her for so long. But as she moved towards the five men she found that half-forgotten techniques and protocols were surfacing. She could do this.

Smoke inhalation. Fortunately no chemical smoke, that could be far more serious. And a combination of burns and smoke inhalation could be dangerous, too.

She shouted a general greeting to the prone men, then told them not to move and she'd check them one by one.

First of all she looked for facial burns, sooty sputum, evidence that the men might have heat-damaged airways. Then she looked at respiratory rates and chest-wall motion. They all appeared to be breathing quite adequately. Well, that was a relief. There would be no need to pass any endotracheal tubes. She went to the medical chest—it was a tremendously well-stocked one—and found a cylinder of oxygen and a mask, which they could share.

Next were the two burned men. The fireman had gently pulled away the scorched clothes from one man's back and bathed the burns with a sterile saline solution. The second man had badly burned hands, which she also bathed. 'Does it hurt?' Lyn gently asked them both.

It did hurt, and that paradoxically wasn't a bad thing. It meant that they were only second-degree burns. Had there been no pain, the tissue would have been damaged beyond repair.

Lyn gave the two ibuprofen as a painkiller, then dressed the burns with a topical antibiotic. That was all she could do in the field. The men needed hospital treatment. She made sure that they were kept warm—even in this heat it was necessary. They were wrapped in space blankets, and she knew she'd have to keep a wary eye on them in case shock set in. But so far...well, it could have been worse.

'If you've got a moment, Lyn,' Adam said behind her. 'I think we have a tension pneumothorax here.'

He was kneeling over the man with the crushed chest, listening with his stethoscope. 'Chest pain, body spasm, anxiety, difficulty in breathing,' he muttered to her. 'Hypotension and jugular venous distension. And no sounds from the left of the chest.'

Lyn knew what that meant. There was now a puncture from the lung into the pleural cavity surrounding it. With every breath, air escaped out of the lung into the cavity—and that reduced the lung's ability to inflate. And now the lung had collapsed.

'There's a good kit here,' she said. 'I'm sure there'll be a needle and cannula. Shall I prepare the site?'

'Please. I'll go to see what I can find.'

'You're going to be all right,' she comforted the man. 'In a couple of minutes you'll be breathing OK.' She swabbed the chest with alcohol then took the man's head so he couldn't see what was happening. It was a large needle Adam was going to insert!

Deftly Adam thrust the needle through the chest wall into the pleural cavity. Then he inserted the cannula, and they both heard the air hissing out from a flutter valve on the end so that air could not be drawn back in—and then Adam strapped the cannula to the chest.

'It hurt a bit...but I can breathe now,' the man muttered weakly. 'Thanks, Doc.'

'You should be OK now,' Adam said. 'Things could have been a lot worse.'

He checked what Lyn had done with the other four men and agreed with all of her decisions. Then the two of them wrote down what they had observed and how they had treated their patients.

She hadn't realised that they had been working for over an hour. She was kept busy tending her patients, making them as comfortable as she could. Now there was nothing to do but wait. This wasn't a hospital, they weren't trying to treat people. All they could do was relieve some of the pain, make sure things didn't get worse and wait for the ambulances.

She thought that she had never worked in a worse environment. The heat she could cope with—just. But the air was thick with dust and ashes, and coated her skin, got down her throat. Next to her was a bottle of lukewarm water, given to her by one of the firemen, and she drank from it constantly.

Then, over the hum and crackle of the flames, she heard the roar of diesel engines. She looked up to see two ambulances slowly pull into the clearing, green-clad paramedics jump out. 'Soon have you out of here.' She smiled at her charges. 'The cavalry's come at last.'

'Rather stay here with you, Nurse,' one of the burned men said with a smile, 'You're better-looking than those ambulancemen.'

Adam was talking to a paramedic, giving him full

details of what had been done. Then the five men were expertly loaded into the ambulances and she and Adam were finished. 'A job well done,' he said. 'Now perhaps we can—'

'Doctor!' They turned to see Jack Leonard running towards them. 'We've got another emergency, a bad one this time.' He looked at them both critically. 'But it's right by the fire, I don't like letting you near. Perhaps, Dr Fletcher, if you—'

'I'm coming with him,' said Lyn. 'We work as a team.'

'And I make all the decisions. All right, you can come. But, remember, if I say move, you do so. That goes for both of you.'

'We'll do as you say,' Adam said, and Lyn nodded. She appreciated that Jack took his responsibilities seriously, was doing his job as well as he could. She respected him for it.

He gave them protective clothing and hurried them across to a smaller vehicle, a red-painted Land Rover. Another two firemen carried the medical chest.

'We're in real trouble now, this wind is all over the place. We get things under control on one front, the wind veers and we have to start all over again. And this wood is like tinder! It can flash faster than a man can run.'

If Lyn had thought that conditions in the clearing were bad, they soon got worse. They jerked down a narrow forest path, bouncing from rut to rut. The sky grew even darker, it appeared now to be raining dust and ashes. A burning twig fell across the bonnet, was brushed aside. The wind through the open window was like a blast furnace. And she could hardly breathe.

'A bird-watcher,' Jack said, with barely concealed anger, 'a twitcher. Waiting till the last possible minute. He thought it would be interesting to observe how the birds dealt with fire. Then he gets into his vehicle, drives like mad and rolls into a ditch. When he comes to he finds he's trapped, uses his mobile to ring for help. He's left it a bit late!' He looked at the sky, watched the wind bending the trees. 'The fire's coming this way. We need some luck.'

The Land Rover came to a halt. Lyn could see a similar vehicle on its side, jammed into a ditch. A fireman waved to them, stepped over to speak to Jack. 'There's no way we can free that leg with the kit we've got. We need the hydraulic jack and mechanical cutters.'

'Where are they?'

'They're being used. We've asked for them and they're being sent, but they're half an hour away.'

Jack looked at the sky, the trees, the redness coming their way. 'The fire will be here before the tools,' he said. 'Doctor, do you want to have a look?'

Lyn slithered down into the ditch with Adam, reached for the medical case and put it handy. Adam was wriggling through the hole where the windscreen had been. He disappeared inside, then she looked through herself.

A middle-aged man with a white beard was looking up at them, remarkably calmly, given the circumstances. He was twisted in a most uncomfortable position. There was blood dripping down the side of his face from a cut in his head. And his foot appeared to disappear into a mass of mangled metal.

'Hi, I'm Dr Adam Fletcher and this is Nurse Lyn

Pierce,' Adam said. 'We're going to see what we can do for you.'

'I'm Dr Jeremy Brice,' the man said, 'but my doctorate is in biology, not medicine. This fire is terrible, no end of creatures are going to be killed.'

'Quite so. Now, I'd like to look at your foot, and then tell me where else it hurts.' Adam wriggled some more, his head now down by Jeremy's foot. Then he pulled himself upright again. 'We'll leave the foot for the moment,' he said with a carelessness that fooled no one. 'Lyn, could you put a dressing on Jeremy's head? A temporary one will do. Any other pains, Jeremy?'

'Fractured ribs,' Jeremy said, with biological precision. 'It doesn't hurt too much until I move. And then it hurts like hell.'

'I'll strap them up.' Adam reached for the roll of plaster Lyn had automatically felt for. 'But first I'll give you something for the pain.'

'I can stand the pain. It's a perfectly natural and useful function.' But Lyn had noticed the whiteness of his face the way he winced whenever Adam got near him.

'An anaesthetic dose,' Adam muttered to her. She drew up some morphine sulphate and handed it to Adam without saying anything. Adam swabbed Jeremy's arm and prepared to inject him.

'You'll feel better after this,' he said neutrally.

Jack slid down into the ditch to join them. 'Can you get that foot free? We have to get this man out in the next ten minutes. The wind is up, the fire is flashing this way, we don't have much time.'

'How desperate are we?' Adam asked, 'because there's no way to free that foot.'

'We couldn't be more desperate.' As he spoke Lyn realised that the heat was, if anything, more intense, the noise of the fire roaring ever nearer.

Suddenly Jeremy worked out the coded messages passing between the two. 'You're talking about cutting off my foot?'

She saw Adam study Jeremy, assess whether he could face the facts. 'Yes, it could come to that. But not for a while yet.'

'I absolutely refuse to give my permission. I'd rather take my chance in the fire. I'll hide under a blanket and it'll pass quite quickly.'

'No, it won't!' Jack shouted. 'See these thickets, these bushes, all this dry dead wood on the ground? It'll flash first then it'll burn for hours. You'd stand a better chance in a furnace.'

'Then that's the chance I'll take. I— Aagh!'

In his excitement Jeremy twisted, and they could see the pain lance through him. Adam took the opportunity to lean forward and inject him. Jeremy's voice became drowsy, the morphine was taking effect. His last words were, 'You are not to take…'

'Is there a kit there for amputation?' Adam asked harshly.

She looked in the box. There was a kit, sealed in a set of sterile bags, tourniquets, scalpels, even a surgical saw. There was also a large bottle of antiseptic. 'There's a kit,' she said, 'but this must be the most unsterile area I've ever worked in.'

'Have you ever assisted at an amputation? You can go now if you want and I—'

'I've told you! I make my own decisions. But, Adam, Jeremy was absolutely clear. You are not to cut off his foot—even to save his life.'

'I know. I could be sued, perhaps I could be struck off.' He turned to Jack. 'Is there a protocol for this? What am I supposed to do?'

'You're not supposed to leave a man to burn to death,' Jack said sturdily. 'If you like, I'll order you to cut off his foot. I'm senior officer here, I make the decisions.'

'I wouldn't dream of hiding behind you,' Adam said. 'This is a decision I take. Now, how long have we got before we must start?'

'I'd say about five minutes. Perhaps ten, I'll go up towards the fire, run back when there just isn't any more time.'

Lyn thought that there was no time already. The air was full of burning debris, the heat almost unendurable. 'What are you going to do?' she asked Adam. 'This decision is too much to ask of one man.'

'Decisions have to be made. I've made mine.' His voice was flat but she could feel the emotion underneath.

'Then I want to say I entirely agree with you.' She held his gaze.

Jack reappeared above them. 'Get ready,' he called. 'There's not much time left.'

Adam pointed at the trapped leg. 'Clean there as well as you can, Lyn, and then swab with alcohol. Then get yourself as sterile as possible and open the kit.' He paused and said, 'There should be a sterile bag there. When the…foot is amputated you are to clean the wound with saline solution and fasten the foot in the bag. It must go with Jeremy to hospital.'

Above them she heard Jack suck in his breath at this. He wasn't as tough as he'd thought. But she was, she had to be.

She did as she was told. Then she poured alcohol over Adam's hands and assisted him in drawing on a pair of gloves.

'There's no one I have more confidence in than you,' he said. Tears came to her eyes, but she said nothing.

Above them they could hear Jack mumbling into his radio. 'We can start when you tell us,' Adam shouted up to him.

'Probably soon,' Jack shouted back. 'But not yet.'

Time passed, seconds or hours—Lyn didn't know. She looked down at Jeremy, his leg bare where she had cut away his trousers, smelled the alcohol she had splashed around so liberally. For a moment she was aware of her own body, the sweat running between her breasts, from under her arms, down her forehead and into her eyes. She looked at Adam. If she was in as big a mess as he was, she must look a sight! But in spite of his discomfort he remained calm, determined.

When would Jack tell them to start? He couldn't expect them to wait indefinitely! She heard the mumble of his radio again. And more time passed.

'Doctor...Doctor...things are getting worse. Perhaps you'd better...start now.' And then, as if saying it would help him deal with the horror, Jack said in a strangled voice, 'Cut his foot off so we can save his life.'

For a moment neither Adam nor she moved. They looked down at the unconscious Jeremy. Then Adam took the tourniquet she offered him, fastened it round the leg and tightened it. She handed him a scalpel. He hesitated.

Lyn remembered a surgeon once telling her that the

first incision was always the worst. There in front of him was naked skin, and he had to cut into it. There was a sense of intrusion, of violation. It only lasted a second, but it was there. Perhaps that was what Adam was feeling now.

'Hang on! Don't start yet, hang on!' Suddenly Jack jumped down into the ditch. She looked at his dirty face, saw an expression she hadn't seen for a while. Was it hope?

'Things are changing a bit,' he said, 'I'm getting reports... Hang on a bit longer.'

Adam carefully put down the scalpel, stooped and loosened the tourniquet. Then he turned to look expressionlessly at Jack. In silence they waited a further five minutes. Jack's radio crackled again, and he turned to look at them.

'Fire's a funny thing,' he said, 'not that I'm laughing much. And fire and wind is even funnier. The wind's veered. And the fire front is now going away from us. You can stand easy for a while longer.'

'You mean we're safe?' She couldn't believe it.

'You're never safe in a fire. But right now it's not coming our way. If we can hang on for another twenty minutes, we'll have the jack and the cutters here. Then we can get him out and carry him to safety. If the wind doesn't change again.'

It didn't seem any less hot to Lyn, but Jack was the expert and she'd take his word. She looked at Adam, hot, sweaty, dirty and still wonderful. He looked back at her, and seemed to read her mind. 'Not everyone can look as professional as you do under these circumstances, Nurse,' he said with a grin. 'Let's check our patient again. I think there's just enough blood getting through to his foot. Otherwise he'd have to lose it anyway. But there's no need to worry about gangrene.'

'He's lucky. D'you think he'll come birdwatching again?'

'Sure he will. He's that type. One of those people who knows what they want, and goes for it no matter what the consequences.'

There was another wait. Then above them there seemed to be no end of vehicles—an ambulance with the green-coated paramedics, another fire appliance. And two men were carrying a great machine down to them.

'The jack and the cutters,' said Jack. 'Would you like to move back a little? Now we've got the right kit we'll have him free in five minutes.'

She noticed that Adam stayed well back, let the paramedics put an emergency dressing on the leg once the foot had been freed. Then Jeremy was lifted onto the road, strapped into the ambulance and driven away.

'I'll give you a lift back to your cars,' Jack said. 'You've done well, but I think we're on top of things now.'

Once back in the clearing Adam phoned Cal, reported what had happened. 'Cal says we're both to have the rest of the day off,' he said. 'How d'you feel?'

'Hot, dirty, tired and a bit weepy,' she told him. 'I'm not used to this high drama.'

He stepped up to her, hugged her, and even though he was as smelly as she was, she loved the feel of him. 'Are you OK to drive?' he asked.

'If we can get away from the heat and smell then,

yes, I'm fine to drive. I'm a midwife remember. We have a hard life.'

'I can believe it. All right, we go back home. But drive slowly and I'll follow you.'

So slowly they drove home. It seemed odd to stop outside her cottage, to see it so clean, so fresh, to see the flowers she had planted round the door. For a moment Lyn just didn't have the energy to get out of the car. The stink of the fire was still in it and she felt that she might pollute the fresh atmosphere if she stepped out. But arriving home was anticlimactic.

Adam appeared at her window. 'Go and get in a bath, lie there and soak and get rid of the smell of fire.' He seemed to be taking charge but she didn't care. He went on, 'I'll go to my place, have a bath myself, organise some food and some wine for us. Leave your front door open. Oh, and take a drink into the bath. We'll both be dehydrated.'

She was happy to let him arrange things. She didn't want to think. She staggered upstairs, left her smelly uniform in a pile on the bathroom floor, ran a long bath full of foam and decided to lie there until some force moved her. And it was good!

She was just going to lie there and not think. When the water seemed to be getting cold she let some drain away, turned on the hot tap with her toe and warmed it up. Today had been too full. She was going to lie here and not think.

After a while there was a tap on her bathroom door. 'Not drowned or gone to sleep? Dinner is served and the wine's uncorked.'

Dinner? Wine? 'You can't have cooked in that time,' she said.

'No need to cook. I've got a phone. I ordered a

take-away. Come on, we've got the banquet. I'll be downstairs.'

Lyn climbed out of the bath, wrapped a large towel round her and ventured to her bedroom. On the landing she could smell the food below and it suddenly hit her. She was ravenous. How long had it been since she'd eaten?

In her bedroom she pulled on new underwear, not worn before. Even for her it was a bit special, a confection of lace that stated rather than concealed. Then she decided that she needed to be even more feminine tonight and put on soft cotton trousers and a pretty top. Then she went downstairs.

She was pleased to see that Adam too was dressed casually in his customary T-shirt and chinos. 'I've raided your kitchen,' he said. 'I've found cutlery, plates and glasses. With a Chinese meal I think we ought to have white wine so I've brought a Sancerre. We can sit and have a civilised meal, be civilised people. I've arranged it that any calls to you or me will be diverted. We are both now, absolutely and completely, off limits. We can think of each other, not work.'

Lyn considered this. 'Let's eat first,' she said.

The meal was marvellous. Afterwards Adam made her sit on the couch with another glass of wine and cleared away the dishes. 'Don't argue,' he said. 'I'm going to wash up. There's hardly anything anyway.'

Five minutes later Adam joined her, his own glass in his hand. She was sitting with her back to the side of the couch, her legs stretched along it, her feet now bare. He sat at the other end of the couch, lifted her feet so that they rested on his knee. 'We're a good team,' he said. 'We work well together. I've said it before, but it's true.'

'You're a good doctor.'

'Possibly. And you're a good midwife. But that's not what I'm saying. This afternoon and this evening, we hardly needed to talk to each other. I didn't need to tell you anything, you knew already.'

She was cautious. 'It happens that way sometimes,' she said. 'It always has with us.'

'We know each other's thoughts. We're a successful team.' He was stroking her feet now, sometimes his hand sliding up to her knees. A gentle caress, but so soothing, so pleasant. 'Do you know what I'm thinking now?'

Lyn lowered her head, decided not to reply.

After a while he went on, 'About Jeremy. How he was willing to risk everything to get what he wanted. Even his life. Now, I think he was mistaken, but we have to admire his determination.'

'I'm glad things worked out for him,' she said. But she knew they weren't talking about Jeremy.

'Perhaps things will work out for me, too. I'm going to forget what you told me, and risk everything.' His voice had altered. Before it had been soothing, now it was harsher.

Adam pulled her legs further over his knees, slid along the couch until he could take both her hands. 'Lyn, I love you. I love you more than I thought it possible to love anyone. I want to marry you, I can't think of a life without you.'

All she could do was bow her head, shake it. No way could she look at him, speak to him.

He went on, his voice more urgent than ever. 'We know each other. I think...I know you feel the same as me. I know you've told me that you can't have children and I won't lie to you and say it doesn't matter. But we can rise above it if we're together!'

It sounded such a good idea. But she knew that she had to...

In a totally different voice he said, 'And, anyway, who says you can't have children?'

It wasn't the question she had expected. 'My O and G consultant. Mr Smilie.' She didn't want to move, but she ran upstairs and fetched the well-thumbed letter. How many times had she read and reread it? She came back to the couch, and this time his legs were stretched out along it. He made her sit between them so her back was against his chest and his arms could hold her.

'I'll tell you before I show you,' Lyn said. 'I love you, Adam, as much as you love me. But we couldn't live together. You want, you need children. Don't try to tell me different, you're one of Nature's fathers. And I can't have children. Here, read the letter.'

His voice was expressionless. 'Someone says you can't have children? That's a big thing to say for definite. But let's see what we've got.'

He held the letter with one hand, the other round her, pulling her close to him. It was warm and comforting.

'Mr Smilie? He's a good man, very kind. I've talked to him once or twice. But he's getting on. I wouldn't exactly call him cutting edge, would you? He's only a doctor, he could be wrong. Did you ever think of getting a second opinion?'

'You're only saying that to be nice to me!'

'No, I'm not. I'm just offering another doctor's opinion. I can see why he reached his conclusions, but I don't see enough to be definite.' He reached over her shoulder, his hand holding a print of an X-ray. 'There are definite problems here, but not as big as they might be.'

'You think I could have a baby after all?'

'Not necessarily. But I don't see enough to condemn you out of hand. Mind if I show these to someone else?'

Lyn shrugged. 'If you think it will do any good. But I suspect that—'

He threw the papers onto the floor, seized her shoulders and turned her so she was facing him. 'That's not the point. Lyn, somehow I've managed without children until now and have been quite happy. I can manage for longer. Certainly I would like them. But I can't envisage life without you. For me that would be a dark end to my life. I love you, Lyn, I want to marry you. So will you marry me?'

'But—'

'No buts! Do what your heart tells you to do. And it tells you to say yes. So I'll ask you again—will you marry me?'

She thought about it. She thought for perhaps five, ten, fifteen seconds. Then she said, 'Of course I'll marry you. And you'll make me the happiest woman in Keldale.'

'How I'll try,' he said.

EPILOGUE

IT RAINED as they lay in bed together that night. Lyn woke to hear the drumming on the window. She slid out of bed to open it, let the rain come through and caress her naked body. The world smelled new and fresh.

Without turning, she knew Adam was behind her. He stretched his arms round her, pulled her back to rest against him. She liked the way their skins rubbed together.

'Things are changing,' he said, 'for the better. For the world and for you and me.'

'Things are changing,' she echoed. 'And they make me so happy.'

They agreed to wait a while before making any official announcement. Not that it did much good.

'You don't have to tell me,' Jane said, 'I can read it in your face and in Adam's. Just make sure you don't get married before Cal and I do. We decided first.'

'We're just seeing each other,' Lyn protested. 'All right, we go out together and we've…we've…'

'I'll bet you have,' Jane said. 'You know, it's something in those cottages. Something in the walls perhaps.'

'We'll just have to see how things go.'

Now that they knew they were in love, it didn't seem to matter that they were moving slowly. They had to get to know each other. Lyn went down to London with Adam, stayed with his friends, saw where he used to work, the flat he had rented out. 'You know I will come down to live with you here if you want,' she said as they sat in their hotel room. 'I'll be happy if I'm with you.'

'I don't think I want to come back, I'm missing Keldale already. The air, the traffic here, they're awful!'

'But what about your TV work? Ros'll be upset.'

'No, she won't. She says she'll be more than happy to work out of Manchester. I can still do the odd programme with her. Even the American programmes.'

That night they were invited to dinner by an old friend of Adam's—Colin Kitt. He was also a doctor, a burly, cheerful man who told her that he was still playing rugby though he knew that he ought to have more sense. 'But I like it, so I do it,' he said.

He took them to a Cajun restaurant in Crouch Hill and she had a meal like nothing she'd ever had in the Lake District.

Surprisingly, Adam seemed a little out of sorts that evening. He was good company—he was always good company—but he didn't say as much as Colin.

'I won't forgive you for taking Adam away from us,' Colin said at the end of the meal. 'We need doctors like him down here. Ah, Cajun coffee.'

Lyn blinked at what came next. A balloon glass spilling over with cream and... She sniffed. 'What's that gorgeous smell?' she asked.

'Alcohol.' Colin beamed. 'How I love it.'

It tasted as good as it smelled, and when she had finished it she felt decidedly happy.

Perhaps this was what Colin had intended. As the glasses were moved away, his voice became more serious. 'I want to give you an engagement present. Adam didn't tell you but I'm a gynaecologist. In fact, I'm one of the best in the country.'

His voice was matter-of-fact, he knew this was true and he wasn't boasting.

'Adam has showed me your medical notes. I know Terry Smilie. He's good, he's cautious, he's caring. But I'm younger, I'm better and, most important, I'm hopeful.'

She could feel her heart hammering in her chest. 'What are you telling me?'

'I want you to come to my clinic. I'll do my own tests, perhaps later on you might have just a small operation. A dye insufflation in your Fallopian tubes. Then...well...it's always a gamble. But you certainly will have a better chance of conceiving. What do you say?'

'Let's gamble,' Lyn said.

Shortly afterwards they got engaged. But there was no great hurry, and there was Jane's and Cal's wedding at Whitsun first. But Adam moved into Lyn's cottage. He had been offered a partnership in the practice and had accepted it at once.

Then it was early autumn again, a year since they'd first met. She was working in the kitchen when he came home, kissed her neck as usual and then perched on a stool in the corner to read his paper.

'I was thinking,' she said. 'You know we said perhaps we'd get married next spring?'

'Whenever,' he said. 'I like spring weddings.'

'Well, I was thinking we might bring it forward a bit. Quite soon in fact.'

He turned a page. 'Whatever you say.' Then he realised what she had just said, threw down his paper and asked excitedly, 'Why? Any special reason?'

'Well, it's early days, very early days.' She smiled at the man she loved with all her heart. 'But if we leave it too late, I might be a bit big for my dress…'

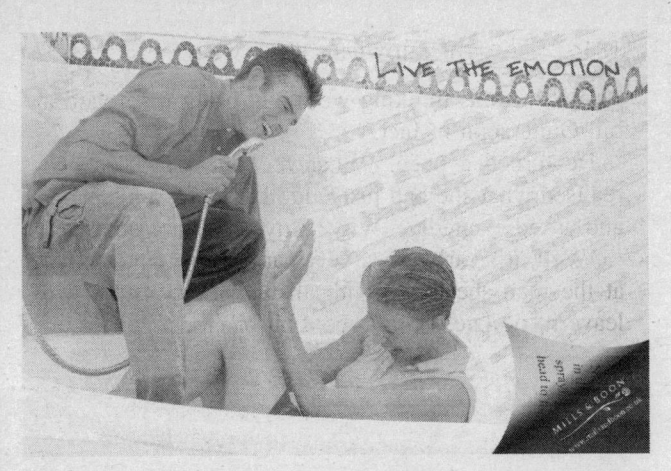

Modern Romance™
...seduction and
passion guaranteed

Tender Romance™
...love affairs that
last a lifetime

Medical Romance™
...medical drama
on the pulse

Historical Romance™
...rich, vivid and
passionate

Sensual Romance™
...sassy, sexy and
seductive

Blaze Romance™
...the temperature's
rising

27 new titles every month.

Live the emotion

MILLS & BOON®

MILLS & BOON

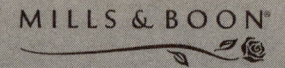

Medical Romance™

TO THE DOCTOR A DAUGHTER *by Marion Lennox*

Dr Nate Ethan has all he needs – a job he loves as a country doctor and a bachelor lifestyle. Dr Gemma Campbell is about to change all that! Her sister has left her with two children – and one of them is Nate's. She must give Nate his baby and walk away – but Nate finds he will do anything to stop her leaving…

A MOTHER'S SPECIAL CARE *by Jessica Matthews*

Dr Mac Grant is struggling as a single dad with a demanding career. Juggling is proving difficult, and he is aware of his son's longing for a mother. Lori Ames is a nurse on Mac's ward – a single mother with a beautiful daughter of her own. Can she bestow upon them the special care that both children so desperately need?

RESCUING DR MacALLISTER *by Sarah Morgan*

A&E nurse Ellie Harrison is intrigued by the ruggedly handsome new doctor at Ambleside. But Dr Ben MacAllister is playing it cool. The pace and excitement of the A&E department thrusts them together and reveals that Ben's growing attraction is as strong as hers – then Ellie realises he has a secret…

On sale 2nd May 2003

Available at most branches of WH Smith, Tesco, Martins, Borders, Eason, Sainsbury's and all good paperback bookshops.

MILLS & BOON

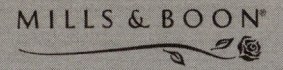

Medical Romance™

DR DEMETRIUS'S DILEMMA by *Margaret Barker*

Eight years ago Dr Demetrius Petros and Staff Nurse Chloe Metcalfe had a passionate affair on the beautiful Greek island of Ceres. It ended when a devastated Chloe returned to England, believing he had never really loved her. Now they are working together – and it's as if they have never been apart...

THE SURGEON'S GIFT by *Carol Marinelli*

Sister Rachael Holroyd has returned to Melbourne City hospital after a traumatic year away – yet the new plastic surgeon manages to make her heart flutter and she finds herself falling for him fast! Dr Hugh Connell is as gifted as he is gorgeous – and he just knows he can help Rachael get over her troubled past...

THE NURSE'S CHILD by *Abigail Gordon*

GP Richard Haslett isn't looking for a wife, and has promised his adopted daughter never to replace her mother. However, he finds himself drawn to Freya Farnham, the new Resident Nurse at Amelia's school. Then he discovers that Freya is Amelia's real mother...

On sale 2nd May 2003

Available at most branches of WH Smith, Tesco, Martins, Borders, Eason, Sainsbury's and all good paperback bookshops.

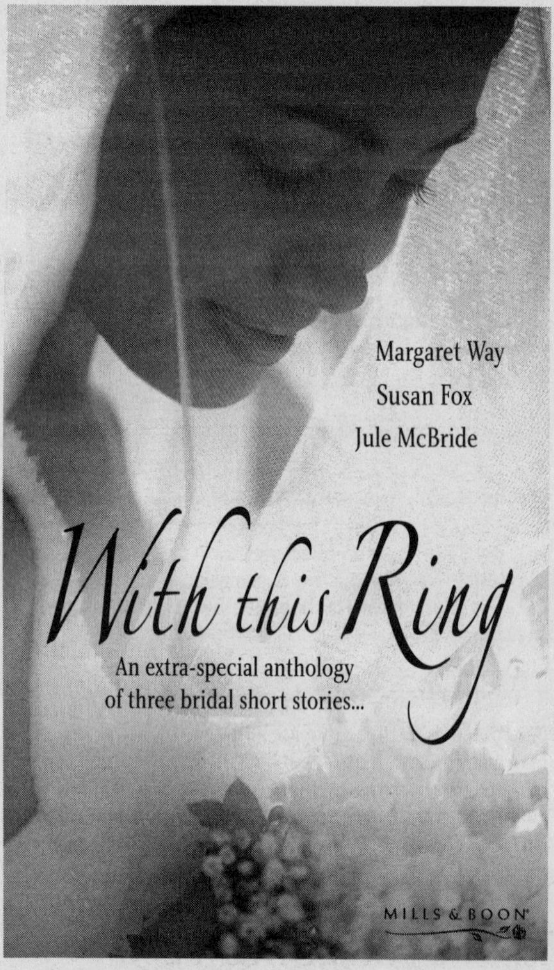
Margaret Way
Susan Fox
Jule McBride
With this Ring
An extra-special anthology
of three bridal short stories...
MILLS & BOON

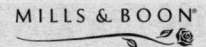

DON'T MISS…

BETTY NEELS

LAST APRIL FAIR & THE COURSE OF TRUE LOVE

THE ULTIMATE COLLECTION

VOLUME TEN

On sale 4th April 2003

Available at most branches of WH Smith, Tesco, Martins, Borders, Eason, Sainsbury's and all good paperback bookshops.

Don't miss *Book Nine* of this BRAND-NEW 12 book collection 'Bachelor Auction'.

Who says money can't buy love?

On sale 2nd May

Available at most branches of WH Smith, Tesco, Martins, Borders, Eason, Sainsbury's, and all good paperback bookshops.

BA/RTL/9

MillsandBoon.co.uk

books | authors | online reads | magazine | membership

Visit millsandboon.co.uk and discover your one-stop shop for romance!

Find out everything you want to know about romance novels in one place. Read about and buy our novels online anytime you want.

- Choose and buy books from an extensive selection of Mills & Boon® titles.

- Enjoy top authors and *New York Times* best-selling authors – from Penny Jordan and Miranda Lee to Sandra Marton and Nicola Cornick!

- Take advantage of our amazing **FREE** book offers.

- In our Authors' area find titles currently available from all your favourite authors.

- Get hooked on one of our fabulous online reads, with new chapters updated weekly.

- Check out the fascinating articles in our magazine section.

Visit us online at
www.millsandboon.co.uk

…you'll want to come back again and again!!

2 FREE

books and a surprise gift!

We would like to take this opportunity to thank you for reading this Mills & Boon® book by offering you the chance to take TWO more specially selected titles from the Medical Romance™ series absolutely FREE! We're also making this offer to introduce you to the benefits of the Reader Service™—

- ★ FREE home delivery
- ★ FREE gifts and competitions
- ★ FREE monthly Newsletter
- ★ Exclusive Reader Service discount
- ★ Books available before they're in the shops

Accepting these FREE books and gift places you under no obligation to buy, you may cancel at any time, even after receiving your free shipment. Simply complete your details below and return the entire page to the address below. *You don't even need a stamp!*

YES! Please send me 2 free Medical Romance books and a surprise gift. I understand that unless you hear from me, I will receive 4 superb new titles every month for just £2.60 each, postage and packing free. I am under no obligation to purchase any books and may cancel my subscription at any time. The free books and gift will be mine to keep in any case.

M3ZEA

Ms/Mrs/Miss/Mr ....Initials......................................
                                                                BLOCK CAPITALS PLEASE
Surname ....
Address ....
....
....Postcode..............................

Send this whole page to:
UK: FREEPOST CN81, Croydon, CR9 3WZ
EIRE: PO Box 4546, Kilcock, County Kildare (stamp required)

Offer valid in UK and Eire only and not available to current Reader Service subscribers to this series. We reserve the right to refuse an application and applicants must be aged 18 years or over. Only one application per household. Terms and prices subject to change without notice. Offer expires 31st July 2003. As a result of this application, you may receive offers from Harlequin Mills & Boon and other carefully selected companies. If you would prefer not to share in this opportunity please write to The Data Manager at the address above.

Mills & Boon® is a registered trademark owned by Harlequin Mills & Boon Limited.
Medical Romance™ is being used as a trademark.